Still Bad for You

Shamar Phillip

Chapter One

Anticipating Mega's return home, Jordyn paced the bedroom floor like a fiend. She knew he was going to be pissed about the baby, but she didn't know what else to do. She couldn't take her back to the daycare because she was afraid of going to jail, and she had no idea where Mila's mama lived, so that was the first thing checked off of her options list. She couldn't ask Polo, because he was dead, and Mega would want to know why she wanted to know where Mila's mama lived, so she had no other choice but to bring the baby with her. To her possible father's house.

"Jordyn?" Mega called out as soon as he entered the house. "Yo?..You in here?"

"I'm upstairs," she answered nervously. "Fuck. Fuck. Fuck," she whispered to herself.

The closer Mega got to the bedroom, the harder her heart pounded in her chest. She almost wanted to hide the baby, until she figured out a way to give her back, but it was too late. Mega was already making his way into the bedroom.

"Ay." He stopped dead in his tracks.

"Surprise?" she questioned her own introduction. "How was your trip?"

"Jordyn?" he asked, as he inched deeper into the room. "Is that...is that, Mila's baby?"

"Yeah."

Mega felt an invisible fist cave his chest in.

"Are you serious right now?" he nearly fell onto the bed. "Why, Jordyn? Why? Where's Mila?"

"I don't know." She kept her voice light. "It wasn't supposed to go down like this at all."

"What wasn't supposed to go down like this!? What are you talking about?"

"My plan." Jordyn lowered her head, feeling ashamed.

"What are we supposed to do with this baby, Jordyn?"

Mega sat at the edge of the bed with his head in his hands, afraid to look at the precious baby girl his girlfriend had cradled in her arms.

"I don't know, Mega. I wasn't planning for Mila to just up and disappear!"

"Well, what exactly were you planning? You done some shit like this before?"

"No! What the hell?" she paced the room as she rocked the baby to soothe her crying. "I was only trying to help and now look! I guess I'm a mom now? I don't know what to do, Mega."

Mila wasn't supposed to leave without her baby. She was supposed to come to Jordyn, call it truce, take her baby and get out of dodge. Or whatever the fuck she did when she wasn't setting up her ex-boyfriend's murder. However, Jordyn's plan backfired and she was stuck with a baby she had zero knowledge about. She thought about dropping the baby off at Mila's mama's house, but something had her clutching to the little girl like she was her own.

"This is kidnapping. You know that right?" Mega shook his head. "How the hell did you even find the baby? And why would you think it was a good idea to bring her here? Come on Jordyn!"

"I'm sorry!" she panicked, still rocking the baby in her arms. "Stop yelling, you're making her cry more. Oh my God, what am I supposed to do?"

Mega raised his eyebrows and shrugged nonchalantly before replying. "You tell me. This was your plan."

It was her plan. One she thought would make life a little easier for him, but all it did was create more friction.

"Mega." She whined, stepping in front of him with the baby.

He didn't have the words. Mega only shook his head, closed his eyes and fell back onto the bed.

"Say something. And you haven't even looked at her one time." Jordyn frowned at her own recognition. "Regardless of anything, there's a possibility that this baby is yours, so you would have had to see her one way or the other."

"Yeah, on MY terms." He got up and headed towards his mini hookah lounge. "You didn't even give me the option of wanting to see this baby!"

Jordyn didn't understand why he was so upset. She knew to some extent, but he was acting like it was a baby he took care of and then found out she wasn't his. Aside from being surprised, Jordyn thought he would have been at least a little happy to finally find out whether she was his or not.

"This is crazy." He laughed and lit his blunt. "I can not believe this."

"Well, are you gonna help me figure this out?"

"Help you figure it out?" he held his hand up to his chest. "Now you wanna ask me what to do? I don't know, Jordyn."

"What if she's yours? Then what?"

"Exactly! Then what!? This is exactly why this," he waved his finger around her imaginary planner, "should've never happened."

Feeling defeated, Jordyn rolled her eyes and went back to the bed to tend to the baby. She told herself she would figure it out, with or without Mega's help, even though she had no idea where to start.

Mega was in a state of terror. There was a possibility of him and Mila having a child, and his new girlfriend was in possession of the child. It blew his mind. He silently hoped and prayed the baby wasn't his. Not because he didn't want kids, that just wasn't how he imagined himself finding out he was going to be a father. Or that he already was.

"Do you think she's mine?" he asked, finally breaking their silence.

"If you looked at her you might be able to tell me." Jordyn replied.

She believed the baby was Mega's. Only because she was head over heels already, and that would be the only reason-other than being a baby-loving her would come so easy.

"Come look at her." She smiled and cooed with the baby. "She's the cutest thing ever."

"I'm good."

Exhaling his smoke, Mega pondered on the kid being his child. That would make his enemy his baby mama and he would then have to think about an alternative option to killing her. To him, that was asking for a lot. Mila smiled in his face everyday and never once mentioned she had a child. And she tried to set him up. That was the ultimate violation. She had to be dealt with. But, how?

"Hello?"

Jordyn's instincts took her ears to Mega's phone conversation.

"Hey Mega," a woman's voice boomed through the speaker phone. "This is Brenda, Mila's... You know who I am. Have you seen her? She was supposed to stop by a few days ago, before she went to work, but I haven't been able to get in contact with her."

Mega was shocked to hear from Brenda. The last time they spoke to each other they were arguing about Mila, and there she was calling like nothing ever happened. He finally saw where Mila got her audacity from.

"Nah. I haven't seen her since the other night. Ask her boyfriend."

There was an awkward silence. Almost like Brenda had something else she wanted to say, but was afraid to spill the beans.

"If I hear from her I'll make her give you a call." Mega spoke up, ready to end the awkwardness.

"Ok. Thank you."

"Alright."

Just before he pressed the end button, Brenda opened her mouth to get her frustrations off her chest.

"H-hey Mega," she let out a gust of air. "I don't know if Mila ever got around to telling you, but you two have a baby. A daughter. Mecca….M.J is her nickname." She smiled thinking about her only grand baby. "She looks just like you. That's why we call her M.J."

Jordyn was staring at Mega with her hand covering her mouth. Her heart was breaking imagining how he must have felt at that moment.

"How old is she?" he asked, almost in a whisper.

"One."

It made sense. Mila was still living up north when Mega found out about another man. After that, they stopped communicating for a while, so he had no idea she was pregnant all that time.

"I just wanna make sure my daughter and grandchild are ok."

"I have the baby." He said, not even thinking about his response.

"Huh?" Brenda shot up in her chair. "You have M.J? How?"

"I'll have to come see you and we can talk about it." He fought back tears. "You still in the same place?"

"Yeah." She frowned, wondering what the hell was going on. "You on your way now?"

"Yeah."

After hanging up the call, Mega sat for a moment. Fighting the reality that fought back to sink in. He had a daughter. By his enemy. As much as he hated it, the news leveled the playing field for them. Mila would have been an easy kill for Mega. But, after finding out they shared a child she had a bit of leverage.

"You ok?"

Jordyn was trying her best to be there for him in a way that wouldn't make him upset, but he wasn't having it.

"Megaaa," she whined again as she bounced M.J on her lap for him to see. "Look how cute she is. And she does look just like yooou." She sang, trying to get him to lighten up.

"I'll be back." He finally replied, keeping his back turned to the both of them. "I gotta go figure this shit out."

Jordyn laid M.J down on the bed and made her way over to her man before he made it out of the room. She wanted to touch him. To feel that he still felt the same about her, even though he was mad at her.

"I'm sorry." She pouted, grabbing his hand. "I really didn't think this all the way through. But, I'm glad I did it. I mean, at least we found out who she belongs to. That counts. Right?"

She was right. It did count. He didn't like how the information came about, but he was glad to know that he had a child.

"You right." He kissed her forehead. "It counts. I'll see you later."

He still hadn't laid eyes on the baby and Jordyn felt a way about that. She knew he was upset, but damn! It wasn't the baby's fault that her parents' relationship was so dysfunctional her mother didn't know who her father was. And Mega was just as much to blame.

"Daddy's being mean." She lifted M.J up to her chest and patted her back. "It's not your fault. Look at you! You're so cute!"

Baby M.J seemed to be liking Jordyn too. She smiled and giggled every time Jordyn said something to her. She even let her change her diaper without too much fuss.

Throughout the day, Jordyn thought about Mega and how he must have been feeling. She wanted to call him a few times, but decided against it. He needed space to get his head on straight, so she spent her time playing with MJ. Rewashing baby clothes. Changing diapers and making lunch. Even though she had no idea what to feed a one year old; before she hopped on Google and became a baby chef guru.

It helped that her daddy ate so much junk food too. He had everything she needed to prepare a simple meal for a baby just starting out on real table food. He also had a pack of baby bottles on hand. Which, she could only imagine what he needed those for.

"You had a good lunch? Are you ready for a nap?" Jordyn asked, as if MJ could answer.

Her jibber-jabber and splatters from spit bubbles was good enough of a reply for Jordyn.

"I gotta get this on video," she laughed and grabbed her phone from the back pocket of her jeans. "You look just like your daddy, girl."

MJ did look just like Mega, with a head full of curls. Little short stubby legs and arms. Chubby feet and small hands. She even smiled like him too.

"I'm gonna have to go get you more diapers. Maybe I'll go after your nap. No!" she quickly remembered Pauline would be coming in from Bingo. "I'll have ma grab some on her way."

As she climbed the stairs to put MJ down for a nap, she thought about what else she might need for a baby. She also thought about what would happen if Mila never came back. She hoped Mega wouldn't give the baby back to the grandmother. Although she did have more of a connection with MJ than he did, Jordyn felt like if her mother didn't have her then he should. He was her father at the end of the day.

Chapter Two

Going to have a sit down with Brenda was the last thing Mega ever thought he would be doing. Especially, with the way they kept their distance from each other after they fell out. He called that woman every demeaning name he could think of, and she did the same. All behind a female who played the game like an almighty champion. Brenda had her sneaky ways too, so he wasn't even mad at Mila. The apple didn't fall too far from the tree.

"Long time no see." Brenda looked him up and down as she welcomed him into her house again.

"Hey, how you doing?"

In his head his greeting didn't come out so dry, but when his ears heard it, it made him cringe a little.

"Where's Mecca?"

"She's safe." He replied, taking a seat on the same couch he once fucked her daughter on.

"I thought you would have brought her with you?"

"I mean, if she is my daughter, I should be able to spend time with her. Right?"

The words poured from his mouth with zero emotion behind it. Mega wasn't ready to accept Mecca as his own just yet, and he certainly didn't trust Brenda. So, he kept his guards up until he knew for sure he would have the chance to be a part of his daughter's life.

"Of course. I just wanna make sure she's alright. Mila too. Have you heard from her?"

"No. And quite frankly, I don't wanna talk about Mila. She tried to kill me. Set me up rather."

"What?" Brenda laughed. "Y'all two been at each other's throats since the day you started."

"Nah, I'm serious. I found out about Polo."

The room grew quiet. Brenda knew about Polo all along and while she didn't care for him too much, she understood the measures of playing the game to get what you wanted. Her mother taught her that and she passed it down to her own seed.

"And what happened with that?" Brenda plopped down in her recliner and lit up a cigarette. "Is that why she went M.I.A?"

"Probably." He shrugged. "Mila took some money for a hit she couldn't come through on. I don't doubt she got niggas on her trail now, and I should be one of them."

Mega gave Brenda a look to confirm he was the hit and saw Brenda's heart shatter through her eyes. He thought she hated him, but after seeing some sort of unwillingly expressed compassion, he felt a little different about the woman.

"Wow." She shook her head. "I can't believe she would stoop that low. I'm really at a loss for words right now. Mila," she sighed, "what in the world has come over you baby?"

If he felt like arguing, Mega would have told Brenda exactly what came over her daughter. The parenting skills of a heartless gold digger is what it was, but he wanted things to be different. MJ made them family, so things had to be different.

"Anyway," Mega detoured the conversation to what he really came to talk about. "The baby. Mecca? What is it that I need to know about her?"

Brenda let out a light sigh before she dove into her tell all. Truthfully, she was happy that MJ belonged to Mega. Had she turned out to be Polo's, her own life would have been a living hell.

"Mila was pregnant when you left New York. She was afraid to tell you, because she wasn't sure if you were the father, or that boy I hate to even think about. That's where a lot of the anger and hostility was coming from between the three of us."

She waited to see if Mega would chime in, but he didn't. His eyes were empty and his ears were open, but his lips remained sealed.

"She didn't find out the baby was yours until a few months ago. Before then, Polo did little things here and there. I knew she was yours though." She smiled halfway. "Mila should have told you a long time ago. There wasn't a day that went by where I didn't want to tell you myself, but that's my baby. I couldn't overstep my boundaries there."

Loyalty was big for Mega, so he wasn't mad at Brenda for holding out on him. Besides, that was something a baby-mama should be the one to tell anyway.

"I respect that." He nodded.

"Well, how are you feeling about all of this? I know it's like being hit out of nowhere, but there's a baby involved here. She needs her mother. And her father."

"I agree." Mega relaxed into the sofa. "I don't really know what Ima do at the moment. I can't even believe I'm somebody's dad. That's crazy."

"Can I….I can trust that my granddaughter is safe with you?"

If looks could kill, Brenda would've dropped dead in her chair.

"I guess we'll see." He replied, getting up to leave. "Hopefully we can both trust that she's ok with me. Ima get up out of here though. I got a few errands to run. I'll let you know If I hear from your kid."

Brenda knew better than to think Mega would ever do anything to hurt a child. He was cutthroat, but she'd seen him with his nieces and nephews enough to know that he had a soft spot for children. He also had a steady stream of available funds coming in, so she knew Mecca would be perfectly fine with her daddy.

Once Mega was inside the privacy of his Jeep, tears of rage and aggression rolled down his cheeks and stain his shirt. He was mad. Hurt. Scared and confused. Although he was more than willing and able to step up and take care of his baby girl, he wasn't ready to be a father. He still had his fists full of the street life, and that wasn't something he planned on letting go of any time soon. It made him even more mad to think about missing the birth of his first born. If trying to set him up wasn't enough of a reason to kill Mila, to him, that surely was.

"Yeah?" he wiped his eyes as he silenced the ringing of his cellphone.

"It's me, Layton. Where you at?"

"Shit! Layton!? Where you at!? It's quiet for the time being."

"They finally released me from the hospital. Can you come scoop me?"

"Hell yeah. I'm on my way."

"Aight."

Layton was Mega's comfort zone. His best friend. The person he turned to when everything seemed to be heavy and out of place. They're so close people often mistake them for being a couple. It didn't bother Mega, and the only time it bothered Layton was when she had to defend her sexuality against it.

He felt himself self-soothing, thinking about their friendship and how she was always there when he didn't know what to do. He was sure she would help him with the baby if he needed it, so he didn't know why he was so iffy about it.

"Booooyy, I thought your ass was a goner!" he joked, hopping out of his Jeep to greet his best friend.

"Shiiiid me too, nigga!"

"I guess you earned your stripes now, Killa."

"Yeah, whatever fool!" Layton laughed as she struggled to get up into the Jeep. "Goddamn! Why you got this damn car jacked up like this!?"

"Cause the hoes love it." He flashed a grinch-like smile and hopped into the driver's seat to clear the parking lot.

Layton was fucked up, but it didn't look like the hitman was really trying to kill her. Internally. He sliced her up a great deal. Broke her hand, so she wouldn't be able to tattoo for a while. Even laid a few good punches to her, but still missed all the major organs and arteries.

Before making it to Layton's house, Mega stopped at the grocery store to grab her a few things for the next couple of days. Doctors said she may experience a lot of pain while recovering and Mega wanted her to be as comfortable as possible when he wasn't there to help.

"You get my beer?" she asked, rummaging through the grocery bags.

"I got you, big dawg. Got you the biggest box I could find."

"Preciate ya."

The car was silent for a while after leaving the grocery store. Mega, was in his head trying to figure out how to tell Layton he had a baby. And Layton was busy on her phone trying to prove to her hoes she wasn't out sleeping around.

"Bruh, females crazy!" she laughed and blacked the screen of her phone. "This damn girl don't believe that I almost just died! She swear to God I was out fucking with another bitch. What the hell man?"

"That's how they be, dawg." Mega shook his head, thinking about all the times he had the same argument with Mila.

"What's wrong with you? You was all hype to see me not too long ago, now you looking all sad and sappy. You good?"

"Man," Mega sighed. "You ain't gon believe this."

"What?" Layton grew nervous. "What happened?"

"I found out Mila had a baby a year ago." He looked over to see if she knew where he was going with the story. "And it's mine."

"Mila had a baby?? Mila Santana?"

"Yes."

"And it's yours?"

"Yes."

Layton scratched her head as if that would help her brain process the information faster.

"How you ain't know she had a baby? Wasn't you blowing her back out every night?"

"Nah. Remember we fell off for bout a year when she was living in New York. I seen her a few times, but she never said nothing about being pregnant."

"Well, where the baby at? That's crazy as hell man."

"Jordyn got her."

"WHAT!"

"Right." He shook his head. "When all the shit went down she went and pretty much kidnapped her, thinking that was gon help the situation."

"AY!" Layton roared with laughter. "That's a real rider right there boy! She kidnapped your ex bitch baby to make her fall the fuck back? That's what I'm talking bout! I know we sisters now. Fuck that!"

"Lay, this shit serious bruh. I got a lil girl."

Layton knew the situation was serious, but it was so ridiculous she couldn't help but laugh. Mega loved kids and he was always talking about having a baby anyway. He had the means to take care of her and even though Mila was a bitch, Layton knew she would take care of things on her end too. So, she didn't really see why Mega had so much doubt about being a father.

"What you gon do? You gotta be in her life regardless. I ain't gon let you NOT be there."

Mega looked at her like she was crazy as hell for bossing up on him like that.

"Don't give me that look. You knew having unprotected sex could lead to this. Yeah, Mila was grimey as hell for not telling you, but what else is new? The baby has no fault in this and besides, I got me a lil niece now. What's her name?"

"Mecca." He nearly whispered.

"Nigga, put some respect on my niece name. Say it with your chest!"

"MECCA." He laughed, feeling lighter about the situation. "You crazy as hell, you know that?"

"I know. That's why we best friends. You got this, big dawg. Don't second guess it. Shit, you see Jordyn gon hold you down through whatever and I always got your back. You need a babysitter, fuck with me. Need diapers, clothes, whatever man, I'm right here with you. Alright?"

It took him a minute to answer, because his voice was full of tears, but once he got himself together again he nodded and took everything in. He had a baby. It wasn't the way he wanted things at the moment, but he had to be there for her. His dad was nowhere to be found while he was growing up and he made a vow that when he had his own children, that road was one he would never turn on.

"I love you, Lay."

"I love you too, my boy. You gon be alright. Mila made some fucked up decisions, but at the end of the day she a real one. She gon do what's right for that baby."

Chapter Three

Jordyn wasn't opposed to owning up to her shit when she was wrong, but she started to feel like Mega was being ridiculous. And a coward. He left the house two days prior and hadn't reached out to her since. Despite the hundreds of times she called and texted him, he hadn't called to check on her. Hadn't called to check on MJ. Hadn't called to make sure no one came by and blew the house up. Nothing. Jordyn was pissed, but she never stopped reaching out for a response.

"This is what? The hundred and twenty-something time I've called you? I don't know where you are, or what you're doing, but this is really fucked up. I know you're upset about the baby, but Mega, she's yours. Deal with it. Nobody told you to be out here raw-dogging Mila. If you would've kept it in your pants you wouldn't be in this predicament. Now call me back. I have to go back to work soon and you're going to have to keep your daughter while I do that. Seriously. Call me back. And you're still the most handsome, sweetest guy ever. Call me back. I'm not kidding."

Jordyn had no idea what to do with MJ. Her mom couldn't babysit while she worked and Kaylani had already done enough helping with the kidnapping. She refused to let herself believe Mega would leave her stuck with his kid, so she continued to wait for him to call her back and do what she had been doing. Which was: be a good girlfriend and mom to his child, while he was out doing whatever it was he was doing.

With baby MJ crying in the background, Jordyn looked around the room for keys to one of the cars Mega had collecting dust in his garage. She also scavenged for any money he may have had lying around. She felt like she was doing something wrong by looking through his things, but she needed it to be able to take care of his kid. She couldn't let the baby go without because he was afraid of stepping up to the plate. That wasn't how she was built.

"I found them, MJ." She smiled, jingling the keys for baby MJ to see. "Now," she picked her up to quiet her cries. "Where does your daddy keep his money? Can you help with that?"

MJ had no idea what Jordyn was talking about, but the way her tiny little fingers pointed out objects around the room you would have thought she did.

"You wanna try over there?" Jordyn asked, following the direction of her finger. "You think that's where it is? Let's see."

Jordyn opened a drawer on the end table Mega had in his hookah lounge and what do you know? There was a wad of hundred dollar bills.

"You are so smart, MJ. Thank you." She kissed her chunky cheek. "How much do we need?" she continued to ask for MJ's input. "Let's take….a thousand. That should be enough to get you everything you need for a while. Right?"

After MJ gave her consent, Jordyn headed to her room to get herself and MJ dressed so they could set out on their shopping spree for baby merch.

Having a kid wasn't so bad, Jordyn thought. As long as you had the money and help with babysitting. They were cute and cuddly. A little loud and restless at times, but other than that, she didn't mind having a little friend to keep her company. Especially, since Mega was missing in action.

"Alrighty," she stood in front of the mirror so they could check themselves out. "I say we're ready to roll, huh? Let's give daddy another call and then we can go."

With her diaper bag on one arm and MJ in the other, Jordyn used her shoulder to hold the phone to her ear while walking towards the garage to see which car went to the keys she had.

Of course, Mega didn't pick up his phone. Again. So, she left another message just as she did the last hundred and twenty-something times she called him.

"Ok, MJ and I are on our way out. She needs diapers and clothes and stuff, so. Don't be mad at me, but I had to look through some of your things to find keys and money. I would've used my own money, but I haven't been to work. You know. I only took a thousand from your drawer in your smoking section, that should be enough. Whatever we don't use I'll put back and I'll make sure I don't crash your car. Call me back when you're ready to talk. Until then, you know where to find us. Alright, I guess," her voice started to crack when MJ chimed in with her giggles. "We'll see you soon."

After taking a moment to get herself together, Jordyn opened the door to the garage and pressed the unlock button on the clicker in her hand. She decided to go with the BMW, because she felt like it was the most safe for MJ's car seat. Also, she didn't know how to drive a stick, so Mega's race car wasn't even a second thought.

Like a pro, Jordyn fastened the car seat into the seatbelt, strapped MJ into it, gave her a bottle to keep her quiet, then made her way to the driver's seat. She was surprised to hear her phone ring while she got herself ready to back out of the garage, because no one ever called her. She was even more surprised to see that it was Mega calling her back. Finally.

"Where are you?"

"I been at Layton's."

"Is she home? Is she ok?" Jordyn asked, genuinely concerned.

"Yeah. They released her the day I went to sit down with Brenda."

"Are you safe?"

Mega felt a sting in his heart when she asked that question.

"I am."

"Am I safe?"

"Yes. You and the baby are safe." He laughed a little. "I would never leave your side if I knew you were in any kind of danger, Jordyn."

"Good. Are you coming home any time soon? I'm supposed to start work again tomorrow, so you're going to have to babysit. If my boss wasn't such a dick I would take her with me."

"You know you don't have to go back to work, right? You proved yourself worthy enough for me to take care of you."

"Are you just saying that because you don't wanna be left alone with MJ?"

"No." He frowned. "The baby has nothing to do with what I said."

"Okay first off, we're not calling her the baby anymore." She lectured. "Her name is Mecca. Or MJ, for short. And ok. I don't know how I feel about not going to work. I'm used to making my own money, but I'm willing to try."

Mega was slightly turned on by her authoritative tone. She never got like that with him before, so he knew she was dead serious.

"Did you get my message about the money? And the car?"

"I did," he nodded. "You don't need to tell me what you took. I trust you."

That made Jordyn smile so hard her cheeks hurt a little.

"Where you going?" he asked, still not acknowledging the fact that his daughter was with her.

"Well, MJ and I," she emphasized, "are going to get baby stuff. So, maybe Target and then the mall? I don't know. I've never been shopping for a baby before."

"Let me know when you get to the mall. I'll meet you up there."

"Mega," she rolled her eyes, "you do know that I have your baby with me, right?"

"I know."

"So then acknowledge her, please? I know it's hard, but she doesn't bite. You don't have to be scared of her, she's just a baby."

"I know." He chuckled. "It's just still new to me. I'm slowly coming around though."

"Good. I'll help you with whatever you need help with, but you gotta open up and work with me."

"I will. I promise."

"Ok. I'll call you when we're on our way to the mall. So smoke. Drink. Do whatever it is you need to do to calm your nerves, so you can have a proper meet and greet with your daughter."

"Got you. I'll be there."

"Ok."

When the call ended, Jordyn felt ten times better. She was afraid Mega would've never come around, so the fact that he was the one to initiate meeting them really meant a lot to her. It also meant a lot because she knew how scared he was. She didn't blame him. Being a parent was a huge responsibility. Especially, living the type of lifestyle he was living.

"Your daddy's coming to meet us MJ," she sang, looking at the baby through the rearview mirror. "This is a big deal, girl. He's so afraid of you. So, we're gonna be on our best behavior, get him comfortable, and then make our way right on into his heart."

When she realized she was speaking for more than just MJ, she smiled to herself and thought about the possibilities. She also thought about how she hadn't shed one tear over Polo being dead. Which was crazy, because she loved him at one point in time. But, after doing the most reckless shit she'd ever done in her life with Mega, he meant absolutely nothing to her. Jordyn had Mega to thank for that. If it wasn't for him throwing all his positive energy around, she might still be stuck in the trap not knowing her worth.

"Where you two headed?" Pauline stopped Jordyn as she got out of her Uber at the end of the driveway.

Jordyn rolled down the window and replied, "shopping. Wanna go?"

"Nah, I'm worn out after bingo. Mega got you out here playing house don't he?"

"Something like that." Jordyn laughed. "My baby's just a little scared that's all. He'll be alright."

"And what about you? How will you be? You can never know a man's true intentions, baby girl. I like Mega, but I don't want you getting your heart hurt behind none of this."

"I'll be fine, ma. Mega has kept it realer than family with both of us, I don't see him changing up now."

"Ok. Y'all be careful on that road. Let me know when you make it to where you going."

"I will. I love you."

"Love you too." Pauline waved them off and headed inside.

Her mama's words drilled her skull until she got a headache. Jordyn hoped like hell MJ wouldn't make Mega want to get back with Mila, but her mama was right. You never did really know. She couldn't be mad at him if he decided to work it out with her. Even though she would be hurt, Mila was the mother of his child. Jordyn always told herself if she had a baby she would want to be with the father of her child, so she didn't expect anything less from Mega.

"Alright, Jordyn." She wiped a subtle tear from her eye. "Enough of thinking negative. Whatever happens, happens. Right MJ?"

MJ replied by clapping her little hands to the music softly flowing through the speakers.

"Right."

Jordyn couldn't get over how cute she was. It had been years since she'd been up close and personal with a baby, and the more time she spent around her the more she wanted one of her own. It even brought back the painful memories of when she was pregnant by Polo.

That was a time in her life she wished would have never happened. He made her get an abortion because he wasn't ready. At the time, it killed Jordyn inside, but the deeper they got into their relationship, the more she realized it was for the best. She was glad she didn't have any ties to that man. She really didn't know why she stuck with him for so long, aside from the money he gave her to keep her from asking questions.

"We're on our way to the mall now." She sent Mega a text after their Target haul. "Meet us in the food court."

Chapter Four

Pauline was crowned Miss America nearly forty years ago. Her demise still haunted her from time to time. Especially when she was alone with too much time to think. Those days, the only things that helped take her mind off of the memories were bingo, making money, and smoking weed. And the cancer she felt like was her ex-husbands fault.

Back in the day, Pauline was a bad mama-jama. She had all kinds of men hanging onto her coat-tail. However, Miss America only had eyes for one man. Charles. A mysterious man hired to be her bodyguard after a death threat from one of her fans. It was love at first sight for the two of them. He fell in love with her beauty and bossy attitude, and she fell in love with his grind and muscle.

Charles was a sweet man before the drugs and his greed for money came into play. Pauline was just a willing participant that got caught in his web of lies. After fleeing the relationship with her youngest, and whatever money she could lift from the grips of her combative husband, Pauline moved to Florida to start a new life. Unfortunately, she had no help and her cancer damn near crippled her. She was out of work. Had no family in the area and no help from the father of her children. So, she had to resort back to what she knew best. Selling drugs to make ends meet.

Before she became Miss America, Pauline was one of the baddest hustlers in the streets of Philadelphia. She vowed strictly to weed, but after learning the ins and outs of Hollywood, she quickly shifted her views to the likes of cocaine, and whatever else those white devils asked her to get her hands on. The money came faster that way, and to her, the high was more euphoric. But, when she finally let her man in on her dealings everything changed. They both became hooked on the drugs, sex and spotlight, and soon enough, Miss America was kicked from her throne with no access to her royalities. Or, her first born.

When Mega gave her a whole pound of weed, to keep her head high and cancer-pain free, she thought long and hard about stepping back into the game. Jordyn had no idea of her past and she wanted to keep it that way, but they needed the money. She felt like a bad mother for having her daughter take care of her, so she saw that brick of green as her way out.

"Talk to me." She answered her burner phone with her feet kicked up comfy in her bed.

"You still in the area? I'm trying to get some bud."

"Nope. I been long gone from bingo. You can catch me there tomorrow. How much we talking? Cause you know I only sell ounces and up. I don't do all that petty shit you youngsters be doing."

"Yeah, I know. I'm trying to get three from you. I hear you got that gas."

"That I do. Give me a ring around 3:00 tomorrow, I'll have it for you. That's gon run you about $900."

"I got it. I'll get up with you tomorrow."

"Alright now."

Hearing those kind of numbers brought a glow to Pauline's face she thought she would never see again. Of course, as Miss America, she was used to bringing in six figures, but for a fallen Queen who was sick and down on her luck that was a damn good pick-me-up.

She pondered on what else Mega had his hands in. Who his connect, or connects were, and how much money he was actually bringing in. She also wondered if he would add her on to his payroll. She had a decent amount of customers to get her started out, but she wanted more. Pauline wanted to be back on top where she was used to being. She also needed more product, so she had to give Mega a call either way.

Mega was on his way to meet Jordyn when Pauline's call came through. His first thought was to not answer, but then he thought it might've been an emergency and gave in to his instinct.

"What's good Paulie D? Everything alright?"

"Yeah, everything's good. I wanted to chat with you about something business related. You got a minute?"

"For business? I got unlimited minutes. What's up?"

"Well, as you may or may not know, I used to do a lil something-something back in my day. With the products and everything. I'm almost out of product now and wanted to know if I could get down with what you got going on. You know. Get me and my baby back right. She's been working so hard and it's about time I chip in."

"You got rid of that whole pack I gave you?" Mega asked, amazement filling his voice.

"Hell yeah! Better ask about me, youngblood. They don't call me Mean Pauline for nothing."

"No bullshit?"

"I'm dead serious. I'm no rookie. I was once the queen of Philly and I want that back."

Mega couldn't believe what the woman was telling him. If you looked at her, you would have never even guessed she smoked, so to hear her talk about being out in the streets slanging and banging was foreign to his ears.

"This shit crazy," he laughed, "I'm definitely with it though. Just no funny shit. And we gotta have a sit down so we can go over the B side of things, that's cool with you?"

"Hey, I'm cool with whatever way you conduct your business. I know how I was back in the day and respect goes a long way."

"No doubt."

"Where you at now?"

"Man," he exhaled, "on my way to meet up with your crazy ass daughter and the baby."

"What's going on with that by the way? The baby is actually yours? Like, you know it for sure?"

"Yep. She's mine. Her grandma confirmed it a few days ago."

Once again, reality hit. Him actually saying those words was like finding out he was the father all over again.

"How you holding up about all this? I know Jordyn's already head over heels for the little girl."

"Yeah she is! That makes it even harder. She ain't letting up about her."

"Yeahhh, that's my baby," Pauline chuckled, feeling proud of the woman her daughter was despite the choices she made in life. "She didn't have her dad growing up, so whatever man she decides to settle down with, you better believe she gon be all about making him step up as a father."

Mega knew she was speaking facts. He could tell that about Jordyn the first day he met her.

"I know. That girl going hard too man."

"Having kids ain't all that bad. Once you get the hang of it you'll be alright. I tell you one damn thing! You make some beautiful babies. I don't know what the mama look like, but that baby is every bit of you. I knew she was yours when I first laid eyes on her. Pretty lil thing."

"Thank you, Paulie D." He chuckled. "She is a cute baby."

"Yeah she is. Well, I'll let you get back to what you were doing. Come find me when y'all get home so we can talk more business. I don't wanna get too deep into it over the phone."

"You got it. I'll see you in a few."

That conversation was music to Pauline's ears. Of course, she wanted more than just weed, but like she said, that was a conversation they needed to have face to face. She'd had way too many prison scares in her life to know better than to discuss the whole nine over the phone.

Being the middle man was going to be something she had to get used to again though. However, Mean Pauline was happy to be getting her feet wet. She was even more happy about the money she would be bringing in. She already had her customers lined up too.

Mega only supplied the highest of grades, so the people she knew from the cancer center, who could no longer afford the supply from the doctors, Pauline already had listed in her little black book. She ran into a few of them at the bingo hall and supplied them with samples, just to get them hooked, after that her phone wouldn't stop ringing. By way of them, and people they knew who wanted to cop some fire weed.

"Jen! We back in business girl!"

Pauline was so excited about her rise back to the top, she had to call her best friend from Philadelphia and fill her in.

"What? You done got you another modeling contract?"

"Really!" Pauline burst into laughter. "They ain't ready for all this sexiness again. But no, not yet."

"Then what is it? You back on the blue dream?"

"Nah. That's been kicked out the door with that no good, dirty dog, Charles. But listen, my daughter's dating this guy who got his hands in all kinda pots. The boy gave me…. you heard me? GAVE ME, a package for self-care. One thing led to the next, and he about to supply my demand."

"You don't think you too old to be slanging?"

"You don't think you too old to be tricking?"

"Tricking ain't never going out of style," Jen playfully sassed.

"Drugs ain't either. Drugs and tricking go hand in hand, so we on again."

"What we talking? You know blue dream is still booming loud out here in Philly. These young bucks got shit greens, so nobody really buying that by the bundle these days. They looking for the most high."

"Well, as of right now we only talking greens. When he gets home tonight I'll figure out the rest, but most likely all of that. The boy is living old time lavish, so I know it's more than that."

"Alright now, you sounding like you ready to run off with some shit. Don't do that to Jordyn's man."

"Oh no, that boy has been too good to me and my baby. He's safe. But you know anybody else would've got it. Quick!"

"Your ass still ain't changed." Her friend laughed on the other end. "I miss you out here Pauline, things just ain't the same without my girl."

"We used to tear Philly up something wicked, didn't we? Maybe I'll take a trip back home to visit after-while. This damn cancer," she shook her head, "it's killing me slowly. I don't know what to do about it. I just know I wanna leave my baby girl with something to work with should it take me out before she becomes rich."

"Oh quit talking like that!" Jen hissed. "Your ass is strong as an ox. Ain't never been through nothing you ain't fight your way out of, so don't you start going soft on me now. I'd lose my mind if I woke up one day and couldn't call you."

"Oh, you'll always be able to call me. I just might not be able to answer." Pauline joked.

"I'm about to hang up this damn phone on you!"

"Alright, alright," Pauline laughed. "I'm getting ready to get up off here anyway. Gotta take these meds and put something on my stomach. Kiss the grandbabies for me."

"Ok. I love you, girl. My friend for life."

"My friend for life."

Jen had been by Pauline's side since grade school. Anything she went through, she never went through it alone because her friend for life was right there with her. When they made their pact they were only ten years old and word is bond, not a single thing changed since that day.

"That's my girl." Pauline smiled to herself as she tracked the hallway towards the kitchen. "My girl for life."

Her fears of dying always got the best of her when she thought about leaving her daughter and her best friend behind. What got her over the hump was knowing that no matter where she ended up, Jordyn wouldn't be left in the world alone. Not as long as her friend for life had breath in her body.

Chapter Five

"This guy has the entire south locked down. Why have I never had a business meeting with him yet?"

"I've been trying to get information on him for the past week. No one seems to be able to tell me anything."

"He's a sexy man too." Bossy admired Mega's Facebook, completely ignoring his right hand. "Where is he from?"

"I'm assuming Florida? He has a lot of family up north and in the Caribbean though. That's really all I can dig up. He's in with some pretty heavy hitters too. However, he seems to be the boss of it all."

"Impressive. Very."

Bossy had his eyes set on Mega in more ways than one. He wanted to know how he conducted business, and with whom. When it came to the drug game, he and his family had a lot of connections, so for there to be a lone-star roaming around reeling in more funds than he did, infuriated him. Though, he was also intrigued.

Mega wasn't your average hustler. He was careful. Smart. Low-key, and rich as hell.

His products' potency measured off the charts too. And because he was capable of cooking his own shit, growing and pressing all of his own needs, he eliminated a lot of the middle man's use. Something Bossy hadn't mastered yet.

"Tell me more." He snapped his fingers. "Come on, feed me all I need to know about him. And don't tell me there's nothing. I want it found and I want it cooked. Steamy."

"There's nothing. Seriously. He keeps it sealed pretty tight."

"I'd like him to see how tight I keep it."

"I don't think he swings that way." Bossy's right hand rolled his eyes.

"Yeah, well, neither did you once upon a time. Bring me Charles. I'll make him show me why I did him a favor and kept him alive."

Bossy knew there would be some use for the hitman sooner or later. He was the only one with ties to Mega through his daughter.

"Mm." He continued scrolling through Mega's pictures as he waited for Charles to be brought in. "This is a gorgeous man. Straight as an arrow though, which is no good for me."

Bossy had been into men for as long as he could remember. But, not just any kind of man. He was intrigued by men with power. Men who look good, smell good, and men who know how to wear a suit. He also had the tendency to go after straight men. Most of the time he was successful in those cases, but with Mega, he knew he was barking up the wrong tree. The chase was still fulfilling for him, though.

"Charles." He smiled, as a bruised and limping hitman hobbled through his door. "How are you?"

Charles gave him a blank stare.

"Happy to be alive? Me too."

"Yeah." Charles scoffed.

"I don't ask too much of you, do I? I feel like I pay you good money to do what you obviously love to do. I make sure you're fed and well dressed. Have all the drugs you can handle, and even got you a little family reunion going on."

"What's this about, Bossy?"

"This is about you. And what you can do for me, of course."

"It always is." Charles replied with a sigh.

"Because I am the boss." Bossy sashayed his way over to his favorite hitman and ran his hand down the side of the man's face. "You remember Mega, right? The guy you were supposed to kill, but failed to do so?"

Again, Charles gave him a blank stare.

"Of course you do. Well, I need him. Not dead, but you know, just for a business meeting."

"You really think he's going to do business with you after not keeping your word on a kill?"

"That's my only concern." Bossy raised a finger to his own lips as he pondered. "What do you think? Should you beat him up and bring him to me, or are you capable of convincing him another way? What do you know about him?"

"I mean," Charles shrugged. "The only thing I know about the guy is that he's tight with my kids and owns a tattoo shop. I couldn't find anything on him when I checked him out."

"Isn't that odd!" Bossy made his way back to his desk and picked up his iPad. "The man has a public business profile right here in my face, but none of his business is able to be found? He must be someone very special."

"Oh, he's special alright. That guy he came with? The other big nigga? I know him. We done a few runs together when I first started out. Guy's a stone cold killer."

"I've heard of him once. He's done a few things for my father. A real scary man." Bossy sarcastically shook in his boots.

"So, what am I supposed to do?"

"Everything you're not supposed to do, Charles. Get me a meeting with this man. I want in with whatever he has going on. I want his connections. I want the money, and quite frankly, I'm growing very impatient. You brought me someone who could have gotten me this information and in turn, took a side deal behind my back. And look how that turned out. She's gone and I have nothing on this guy."

Charles started to grow a little frightened. He knew when Bossy became frustrated, nothing ever went as planned.

"So, here's the thing Charles," the room darkened as Bossy's guards piled inside his office and circled Charles like prey. "I want the girl. And I want the man. Mostly for business purposes, but if any other opportunities present themselves, I'm not opposed. And I want them STAT."

On the streets, Charles felt like he could overpower his queer of a boss. Although Bossy was cold blooded and cared nothing about ordering a hit, or pulling a trigger, he was scrawny. And sweet. Very sweet. If it weren't for the bulldogs he kept in his pocket, Bossy would've been in a grave a long time ago with the way he talked to and treated Charles.

Charles had been wanting to get out from under Bossy's family for the longest. Unfortunately, when Pauline left and took everything he had stashed away, he became indebted. When Bossy's dad was killed he thought for sure he would be next up, because Bossy was gay, but that didn't turn out how he thought. Bossy gained the throne and he was kept as nothing more than a do-boy.

"You know what happens when I get annoyed, Charles. We've been here many times before. I'm not my father. So, whatever way you two conducted business during his time, whatever agreement you two had with each other," he waved a finger in the hitman's face. "That's long gone. This is my empire. I call the shots. All of them. So when I say do something, and do something right, that's what I mean."

"Got it." Chalres gulped.

"Do you? Because this little side deal you hustled up has done nothing more than put you more into a hole. You should be dead right now. You should've been dead when Mega asked you to be, but look at me." Bossy rolled his eyes and snapped his neck, "doing you a favor once more, no matter how much money you owe me and my family."

"Come on Bossy, you know it's not like that. I told you what happened to my money."

"Yeah well, that's something you have to deal with, my friend. But the side deals, on my dime? That's a big problem."

"Just give me some time. I can get the girl and the money back. Believe me." He pleaded for his life.

"Oh you better. If not, I promise I'll kill you myself. For real this time. Now, aside from what we already know, and what everyone keeps telling me, what do we know about Mega? Where is his home? Where is his tattoo shop? Who is he dating? Does he have any children? Tell me something."

"He lives in West Palm Beach. His tattoo shop is there. It's the one all the high ends go to. You know, the one by that club you like to go to. This guy isn't easy to get next to, though. It doesn't matter what we know about him, he's untouchable." Charles admitted.

"Who is he dating? And does he have any children?"

"He's dating my youngest. I don't know about any children."

"Can you talk to her?"

"I doubt it. She hates me now. And with good reason."

"I bet it is a good reason. You're a monster, Charles. What kind of man tries to kill his own children? You know what they say: a man who doesn't do right by his own kids." Bossy shook his head as the finishing of his statement.

Charles knew that to be true. He had nightmares about it. He often wondered what his life would be like if he had kept his family together. Seeing his peers in passing with their wives and children made him feel guilty all the time. He knew Pauline, Layton and Jordyn were never coming back to forgive him, especially after the stunt he pulled.

"I should visit his shop. Correct? Or is that too pushy?"

"Are you getting a tattoo? I mean, a serious businessman like Mega, would probably want to discuss nothing but tattoo's in a tattoo shop."

"You're right! Mr. Smarty-pants. How do you suggest I go about talking to him?"

"About what you wanna talk about…. I'm not sure. I just don't see him giving up his routine for someone who didn't keep their word with him. He came to you respectfully, before making a move that was in his best interest, and you still shitted on the guy." Charles admitted.

"Ah ha!" Bossy squealed. "You sure know a lot about that, don't you!"

"I'm just saying."

"You do a lot of 'saying' and not enough doing. Can I trust you to actually do what I ask this time around? Because I'm really at my witts end with you and this sneakiness. Or, should I save myself the trouble and kill you right now?"

"Give me a week. I'll get some information on him and find the girl."

"A week!?" Bossy let out a high pitched scream. "I guess a week is enough time. Don't disappoint me, Charles. Again."

"I won't."

It took everything in him not to pound his hammer of a fist into Bossy's skull. He knew better than to try anything with his goons around, but if they were alone, Bossy's head would've been on a platter.

"Do you need money for travel? Food? A place to stay while you're working?"

"I got a little savings, but I'll probably need more for the travel and bribery."

"You're lucky you were once my father's best friend." Bossy scolded, as he opened his safe to retrieve some funds for Charles to live on over the next week. "You're almost a million in debt. How do you plan on paying that off, Charles?"

The hitman hated when Bossy called him by his first name. He always said it like they were intimate with each other at one point in time, something Charles would've never even thought twice about.

"I could work it off."

"You could, if you knew how to do your job without all the extras. I don't trust you to do anything outside of what you're doing now. So, that's not going to work for me. However, there's no time for that kind of talk right now. We'll figure something out once all of this is taken care of. Now run along. And don't come back without the girl."

Charles hoped Bossy wasn't getting any of his kinky, fetish-y ideas. If that was the case, he'd much rather be put out of his misery right then and there.

Chapter Six

When Mega got to the mall, he sat in the parking lot trying to gather his nerves before entering. His first real interaction with baby Mecca was right ahead of him, and he was nervous about it. Jordyn, on the other hand, was acting like she'd known MJ all of her life and everything was a breeze. He figured it was a woman's intuition or something, because by the time he got out of his Jeep he was sweating bullets.

When he finally entered the food court he saw Jordyn sitting with her back facing the doors. He thought about turning around and telling her to meet him at home, where he had some weed to smoke, but realized either way he'd still have to see the baby. So, he pulled up his big boy pants and headed all the way in.

The closer he got, the more he started to sweat. However, he knew that having Jordyn there to push and guide him would make things a little easier, even though she had no idea what she was doing herself. All she cared about was him having a relationship with his daughter.

"Hey." He walked up to the table with his hands in his pockets.

"Hey." Jordyn smiled at his nervousness. "Say hi daddy." She squealed while bouncing MJ on her knee and kissing her cheek.

The way Jordyn handled MJ, like she was her mother, made Mega's heart flutter. He also laughed a little on the inside, knowing that if Mila saw the shit she would have a fit and cuss the both of them out.

"Sit down. Why are you standing up over us like you about to run up out of here or something?"

"I don't know." He laughed a little as he sat down. "Just nervous. And look at you," he kept his eyes focused on Jordyn the entire time. "You're cute with a baby."

"And MJ?" she asked, brushing him off. "She's cute too right? I did a good job getting her dressed?"

"Yeah you did. You're kinda good at this mom thing. You sure you don't already have some kids hiding out somewhere?"

"Really?" she laughed, rolling her eyes. "I'm sure of it. Maybe I'll have some one day. If you get your act together."

"Oh yeah?" he smiled flirtatiously. "That's on me, huh?"

"As of right now, yes. You're my man, right?"

"We never discussed it. It just kind of…. happened that way, right?"

"It sure did. I wasn't expecting this at all."

Mega wasn't expecting a baby, but there she was.

"How come you didn't know about Mecca?"

"Shit." He exhaled heavily as he leaned back in his chair. "I don't even know. Mila's mom said she was pregnant while they were still in New York. During that time we weren't even speaking because of," he paused, starting to remember the way his heart felt when he found out Mila was cheating on him. "Man, I don't even know." He shook his head. "Shit just crazy."

"Well, tell me about it. Let's get it out there. I mean, that's the only way you're gonna be able to feel comfortable with the situation. You can't keep everything inside forever, Mega."

The way she nurtured him turned him on. She was so sexy to him, sitting across the table loving and coddling a baby she had no ties to, except through him.

"You're right." He smiled at her, seductively.

"So, tell me about it." She said, while feeding fussy MJ her ice cream. "Look at her!"

"She's impatient."

"Mhm. Just like someone else I know."

"Well," he started, after reaching across the table to snag a sip of Jordyn's drink. "I met Mila when I was up north. We hit it off pretty good, even though we both had our own things going on at the time."

"Like…. Yal were both in previous relationships?" Jordyn cut in.

"Yeah. I wasn't really committed to anyone, just talking. I guess. She was though. Her and old boy had been dating for years before we met."

"Yeah, I realized that." Jordyn scoffed.

"Yeah. At one point we decided we would drop our flings and be exclusive. Long story short: I was. She wasn't. I found out and left her alone. Moved to Florida and didn't speak to her for over a year. Now this." he motioned towards MJ.

"Did you always have your tattoo shop? Like, before you moved?"

"Yeah I did. I spent a lot of time in Florida before I decided to move here. I was always back and forth doing business. That's why I respect Layton as much as I do. She held it down whenever I was gone. That's my dawg."

"Did you tell her you have a baby?"

"Yeah I did, thinking she would side with me, but she acting just like you."

"Good!" Jordyn laughed. "I'm glad somebody agrees with me. What about your mom? Did you tell her yet?"

"Nah, not yet. I know she gon flip when she finds out. I don't even know how to tell her."

Jordyn could tell his mama was very overprotective of him. It showed in the way she interacted with anyone he had around. Very cautious.

"I don't know either. She might be mad. That woman is very intimidating."

"Sometimes she is." He chuckled. "She's cool though."

Jordyn took notice of how much more Mega was looking at Mecca. Before, she couldn't even get him to sniff the air in her direction. But, after some time, she had them sitting across the table from each other and Mega had even smiled at her a couple of times. She knew it was the cuteness that was wearing him down.

"You wanna hold her?"

Mega looked at Jordyn like she had asked him to get married.

"Stop!" she laughed. "Just hold her. You're gonna have to anyway."

"Right now?"

"Yes, Mega. Right now." She got up to hand him his baby. "It's not hard. Just hold her like you're holding something important and you don't wanna drop it."

Mega knew how to hold a baby, but it was a different feeling when the baby was his own.

"See! Awwww." Jordyn cooed. "Look how cute y'all look together! I gotta take a picture."

One picture became a collage. And the collage became a video. She took so many pictures, Mega eventually started flying MJ in the air like a baby airplane. Jordyn was so awe-struck seeing him play with his baby she had tears in her eyes. Partly because she thought he would never come around, and the other parts were her wanting that from her own dad and also wanting to share that experience with Mega.

"She looks just like you." Jordyn smiled while she scrolled through the pictures she took.

"You think so?" he asked, taking a long look at MJ. "She looks like Mila, a little."

"She does." Jordyn agreed. "But, that's all you. Spitting image."

"I guess she does."

They sat in the food court another hour or so, talking, eating, and letting MJ play on the merry-go-round before Jordyn was ready to finish off her shopping. MJ was worn out, sleeping in her stroller, while Mega pushed and followed Jordyn around the mall.

"I can not get over this," she laughed. "You are so adorable pushing this baby around in this stroller."

"Shut up." He laughed. "I can't believe it myself. I thought I would only be an uncle for the rest of my life."

"You never wanted kids?"

"Nah. Not really."

"Why not? You never thought about settling down with a wife and kids one day?"

"Sometimes I did, sometimes I didn't. I don't know."

That was a little weird to Jordyn. Mega seemed like the kind of guy to want that type of thing, but then again, he was a hard book to read. One minute she thought she had him figured out, and the next minute she realized she had him completely wrong. He kept her on her toes and that was what she loved about what they had going on.

"We need to get her a crib so we can set her up a room."

"Ok, we can do that. But, why didn't you order all this stuff from the house?"

"Because I got tired of sitting in the house. And I didn't even know that type of stuff was possible."

"You never ordered anything online before?"

"Well yeah, but…. I don't know. I guess I wasn't thinking about all that."

"It's ok baby." He leaned over and stole a kiss from her. "I appreciate what you did do."

When Mega said and did sweet things like that, Jordyn felt like she was on top of the world. She also felt turned on. It was crazy to her that he was such a rough-neck on the streets, but in his intimate life he had a heart made of cotton balls.

After nearly another two hours of walking through the mall, Jordyn was finally ready to go. She bought shoes. Clothes. Toys. Hair supplies. Anything a little girl could ever want or need. She even made a few orders for delivery while they were there. Mega didn't mind spending the money, as long as it meant he didn't have to do the shopping.

"Where y'all going now?" he asked, after buckling MJ into her carseat.

"Uhhh, home? Where else are we supposed to be going? I was gonna cook. Are you coming home tonight?"

Those words stung Mega's heart a little bit. He felt bad for not coming home the last few nights, so he made it his business to be home then.

"I'm following you." He pressed up against her and kissed her lips. "What else you doing tonight?"

"Mmm," Jordyn bashfully bit her bottom lip. "I haven't decided yet. We'll see how nice you are to me later."

"I'll do you a solid. Since you've been taking care of Mecca for me, I'll cook and cater to you so you can relax. I'll even take care of her if you want me to."

"You should be doing that anyway, but it's ok. She keeps me busy, since you said I can't go to work." She playfully sassed.

"Ahh man!" Mega laughed. "I didn't say you couldn't work. I would just like for you not to."

"I bet. So you can keep me all to yourself?"

"Precisely."

After opening and closing her car door for her, Mega started making his way to his jeep. He felt lighter after this outing with Jordyn and MJ, but he also felt strange about it because Mila was still missing in action. He knew she would surface sooner or later, he just hoped it wasn't in the form of a corpse.

MJ helped him make the decision to call it truce with Mila. She was the mother of his child and Mega was a strong believer in children needing their mothers in their lives. He remembered the days he lived without his mother when he was a kid. She was all he longed for. No matter how much fun he may have been having living somewhere else there was never a time when he didn't think about being home with his mom.

"Yo Lay," he called Layton once he was on the road.

"What's up?"

"You ain't heard nothing from Mila?"

"Why would I hear from her? You know that damn girl don't fuck with me."

"Yeah I know."

"What happened? The baby make you have a change of heart? I see the lil pictures ya girl posted. Yall cute."

"Yeah man," he chuckled. "Cute lil thing. As far as the change of heart…. Yeah. I mean, she is my baby mama. I don't want nothing to happen to her. You know?"

"I feel you. She still can't be trusted though, so whatever it is you got in mind, just be careful about it. That girl is crazy!"

"I know. And I know it's gotta be somebody after her for that money. I just don't know who it is. I definitely don't trust Mila, but she does need to be here for her baby."

"No she don't." Layton said, plain and simple. "Jordyn looks like she got all this shit under control. Shit, she got your ass to get with the program. I'm sure she's over there running shop, doing the damn thang."

"Ay!" Mega laughed. "she's definitely doing her damn thang with this shit! That girl wild! She ain't playing no games, but you know Mila ain't gon go for that. She ain't fina let nobody out-do her. Especially when it comes to me and her baby."

"That's true. I don't know what your ass got in them briefs, but it sure does make some crazy bitches."

"Whatever fool. How you over there holding up?"

"Oh I'm good. Mad I can't be at the shop, but I'm good. Just resting."

"Cool. Well, I'll keep you posted on what's going on. Let me know if you need anything."

"I will."

Chapter Seven

New York was the last place Mila thought she would ever end up again. She'd done so much grimey shit to people she didn't even feel safe in her own hood. But, she figured if she was going to be put down, it was better it be by someone from around the way than Charles.

"Think Mila. Think." She lectured herself as she sat inside a half filled Chinese Buffet. "How the fuck are you gonna get yourself out of this one?"

When it came to trouble, Mila was the only mastermind, but for some reason she was stuck on which way to move. Thoughts of Mega flooded her mind. The Hitman. Bossy. Even Jordyn crossed her mind a time or two. She kept telling herself to give the girl a pass, but the stunt she pulled at the daycare just kept eating at her ego. Jordyn had already stolen her man, so it would be over Mila's dead body that she got to keep her baby too.

"What's up ma?" Mila finally answered her mother's call.

"I've been calling you and calling you! Then I had to hear from your auntie that you're back in New York? What is going on, Mila?

Mega has MJ and doesn't want to bring her home. He came to see me and said you tried to set him up?" Brenda paused to catch her breath, while Mila rolled her eyes at her mother's rambling. "Ever since you were a little girl you've been giving this world all kinds of hell. I know I made some fucked up decisions in my day, but you're supposed to be better than I am. Got me paranoid thinking someone is watching my house. I haven't seen my grandbaby. Hell, I won't be surprised if I die from a heart attack dealing with your shit."

"Ma," Mila sighed. "I really can't take all of this right now. I'm in some real serious shit. I fucked up. I fucked up bad, and I don't know what I'm gonna do. I don't even know where to start. I had to come back home to make sure I was safe for the time being. Just until I figure out what my next moves are."

Those words sent a cold shiver down Brenda's spine. She was used to her daughter making moves, but not when her life was at stake. Thoughts of having to bury her only child came barreling into her mind like a freight train hot from hell. Truth be told, Brenda thought that day would have long passed because of the way her child lived her life. Everyday was like its last for Mila. Always had been. And from the looks of things, always would be.

"Look ma, you need to consider getting out of town for a while."

"What? No. I can't leave my grandbaby here alone."

Tears started to form in the pits of Mila's eyes. Every time she thought about MJ and what life would be like for her in the future, it made her sad. She hated herself for the way she chose to live. Knowing that her choices could possibly affect the livelihood of her daughter was too much for her to bear.

"She's with her daddy." Mila replied, forcing herself to swallow the lump of pride that grew in her throat. "And even though I can't stand his new girlfriend, I know she'll make him be the man Mecca needs him to be. The man I wanted him to be."

Brenda was still stuck on the fact that her daughter told her to get out of town. Those words made everything all too real for her. She'd never been the type of woman to back down from a fight, but she'd gotten up in age and her fighting days were long gone.

A sense of urgency washed over Brenda as she held the phone to her ear in silence. She felt like she needed to be with her daughter, wherever she was. Her and baby Mecca. The last time she saw them being the last time she saw them didn't sit right with her. Brenda was ready to pack up what little she could carry, grab her grandchild and hit the road that same night.

"Where you staying? I can get up with Mega, grab the baby and be on my way right now. Whatever you've gotten yourself into, I'm right here with you. We can fight it together. The three of us."

It had been a while since Mila wore a smile on her face. She was thankful for her mother's words and encouragement, but her fight was hers and hers alone. She couldn't fathom the thought of putting them into any more danger than she already had. If something happened to either one of them because of her, she would never be able to live with herself.

"I can't say where I'm at right now. Just know that I'm safe and figuring things out."

"Well, who's after you? Mega? He sounded like he was ready to settle things once I told him that MJ was his."

"I owe some people a lot of money, ma. $250,000. Mega is the least of my worries at the moment."

"Well, why don't you ask him for the money? You are the mother of his child."

Brenda had a point. One that Mila didn't think would get her anywhere, but she had a point. She could ask Mega for the money and even though she knew he probably hated her guts, if her debt was still payable, he would pay it for the sake of their child.

"I don't know ma," she sighed. "Maybe."

Her words were cut off by a sight she never saw coming. Mila knew it wouldn't be too long before someone showed up to collect what she owed, she just didn't think it would've been so soon. Her tracks out of town were covered before anything. She never said where she was going to anyone, so for the Hitman to be stomping around on Brooklyn turf caught Mila off all of her guards.

"I gotta go, ma. I'll call you back in a few days."

"Wait! What's going on?"

Before Brenda got an answer to her question, Mila ended the call and ducked down into her booth. Charles was right outside the buffet she hoped would hide her, with his phone in his hand. She could see his reflection on the napkin holder sitting on the table. It looked like he was waiting for someone to call and give him the "okay" or something.

"How the fuck did he find me already?" she asked herself in vain.

Mila had no issues with squaring up with a man. She'd been there several times with Polo, and each time he got what he deserved. However, Charles was too big for her to fight off alone and she was too far from her car to grab her gun. So, she had no other choice but to wait until the coast was clear. Either that, or she could have asked one of the yellow-faces to create a distraction for her to escape through the back. A plan she knew was a dead end before it even started. The Chinese people were so tired of the blacks in their area they wouldn't help her even if she paid them to.

It was just her luck Charles walked away from the building when his phone rang. As soon as she saw his feet touch the street she jumped from her hiding spot in the booth and hauled ass towards the furthest exit in the buffet. It led out to an alley behind the building where a bunch of dope fiends were crouched over getting high. Something she didn't miss seeing at all. It definitely wasn't a sight she wanted her daughter to see. The thought alone made her sick to her stomach.

"Fuck." She cursed herself as she paced back and forth in the alley. "I do not want to call this nigga."

Mila was all out of options. The Hitman was hot on her trail and the only person she could even think of to back him off was Mega. The amount of power and fearlessness he had made him seem like the devil himself.

After fighting with her heart and her mind for what seemed like eternity, Mila finally gave in to her only option.

"Fuck it."

She dropped all of her pride, dialed his number, and let the phone ring. It rang until his voicemail picked up. Something she knew would happen. It actually surprised her that he didn't have her number blocked. There were times where they were only arguing about another nigga and he blocked her number and all social media accounts. She thought for sure her putting a hit out on him would be the straw that broke the camel's back. However, she was happy to know she could still get a hold of him.

"I know I'm probably the last person you wanna hear from right now. I won't even try to apologize for what I did because I know it's unforgivable. But I need your help. Call me."

Chapter Eight

Mila's text came through while Mega and Paulie D were in the kitchen cooking and talking business. They seemed to be doing more talking than cooking and Jordyn was growing impatient with hunger. She didn't complain too much because she was busy taking care of MJ, but made it a point to let Mega know that she was hungry. And not just for food.

"Queen of Philly, huh?" Mega questioned while he stirred his signature wing sauce. "I heard a few things on the streets about her as a kid. Never knew I'd actually meet up with her one day."

"Wasn't what you expected, huh?"

"Not at all. I mean, I can still see the fire behind your eyes, but you definitely threw me for a loop." He laughed a little.

"And that's exactly what you want when you're hustling. Never draw too much attention to yourself. Always try to stay as inconspicuous as possible."

Mega nodded his head at the woman's advice. It wasn't something he didn't already know, the reminder was just potent enough for him to agree. In fact, his own mom was the one who taught him the code of the streets, and Pauline's advice was on the top of the list. Never draw too much attention to yourself. Too much attention only brought one or two things: Cops. Or Robbers.

"I've been out of the game for a long time now, but I know you have to have your hand in more than one pot to be living like this."

Mega already knew what Pauline was getting at. He'd never disclosed what products he had on hand to her, other than green. That was rule number one on his list. Never give out too much information on yourself because you never knew who you could actually trust.

"I make a few moves." He humbly admitted. "I think you already know which moves bring in the most dough."

"I knew it." She chuckled. "Great masking strategy too. The green can get you started, but the white takes you the furthest. That was always my motto at least."

The Queen of Philly kept replaying over and over in Mega's head. He had his own connects, dealers, and runners, but talking to Pauline made him wonder how much further he could go if he had her on his side. Her making a comeback would be major. Not only for her, but him as well. The amount of bells his name would ring if the upper echelon knew he was the one who brought the Queen out of retirement would be phenomenal.

His only concern was her health. He didn't want to put too much strain on her being that he ran such a tight ship, but if she could handle it he was all for it.

"What you think? You wanna get down?" he finally asked.

Pauline stared at him for a moment trying her damnedest to read his eyes, but saw nothing. No doubts. No lies. No truths. Mega was a complete mystery to her. And anybody else who tried to read his intentions. That was the way he liked it and always intended to keep it.

"How much we talking?"

"Before all that, I'll have to show you around first. Let you in on how I operate and get shit done. I don't sell to no small fish, or local druggies. I work around the heavy hitters and pushers. I'm talking about the niggas who supply entire citites."

Pauline felt that old flame inside her growing hotter and hotter. The way Mega talked about his business gave her the chills. He sounded just like her when she was taking trips out of the country to supply her suppliers, or having her shipments brought into the states on ships and private planes. A real Gangster.

"I respect that," she nodded. "I might even still have a few of my old connects on hand."

Mega liked the sound of that. Pauline's connects were from the 80's and the best of the best. If Mega made his way in with the old heads he could do away with his own connects and become even bigger than he already was.

"You think you can get in touch with your old heads?" Mega asked, with great interest.

"A couple of them have probably passed on their empires by now, but I still have one in my pocket for sure."

"Shit, if I can get down with someone from your era that would be a major move. I don't wanna work with no middle-men though. I wanna be at the hip with the source."

They both got quiet when they heard Jordyn coming down the stairs with MJ. Pauline tried to keep her daughter as far away from her business as possible. Mega already knew how Jordyn felt about him being the dope man, so it was best they kept things between them on the low.

"I guess I'm gonna have to order me and the baby a pizza?" Jordyn sassed as she walked into the kitchen with MJ squealing on her hip.

"Here she go." Mega laughed and rolled his eyes. "I just finished air frying the wings. I like mine fried hard, so it took a lil longer."

"I bet."

Jordyn saw a look on her mom's face that she hadn't seen in a long time. A look she knew all too well. No matter how hard Pauline tried to hide the fact that she was a drug dealer, the joy in it always showed on her face.

"You falling in love with this baby, aren't you?" Pauline asked, taking one of MJ's tiny hands into her own.

"Head over heels." Mega chimed in while he tossed their wings in his signature sauce.

"Is that a problem? She likes me too."

He stared at her for a moment, unsure of how to answer. He didn't want Jordyn getting too attached because he knew how Mila could be. There was no telling if she would even allow him to keep seeing MJ, let alone Jordyn. He also didn't know what he was going to do about Mila. When he finally checked his phone and saw her text he felt something. Something old, and also something new.

The feeling was very familiar, even though he didn't really know what it meant. It made him feel bad for wondering, because he was with Jordyn, but he couldn't help the way he felt.

"Seems you two have something to discuss," Pauline chuckled. "I'm gonna go set the table and take a puff of my spliff while y'all do that."

Jordyn laughed and shook her head at her crazy mama. The woman seemed to be in a completely different headspace being around Mega. When they were home all she thought about was her cancer and when she was going to die. It was a good feeling for the both of them to be out of their walls of misery, even if it was just for a little while.

"So." Mega cleared his throat after downing a shot from his favorite shot glass.

"Before you start." Jordyn stopped him by leaning in to hand him MJ. "I think it's about time you held your baby. And look!" she giggled, "she's even reaching for you."

An involuntary smile crept across his blushed face as he reached in to take his child. As soon as she made it into his arms she let out a loud scream filled with joy and toyed with the chain hanging around his neck.

"Awww!" Jordyn cheesed. "You would think she already knew who you were."

As he cradled his daughter in his arms, lightly bouncing her up and down and kissing her chubby cheeks, he thought about Mila and her text. There was a worry in his heart for her. Something inside him wanted to rush to her to make sure that she was safe, even if it were only for the sake of their child. But, there was also something in him that wanted nothing to do with her.

He was torn between his heart and his mind, and didn't know why. Whatever it was, he hoped Jordyn could help him figure it out before either of them got hurt in the process.

"Mila texted me." He blurted out while she got the wings ready to serve.

"What'd she say?" she asked, keeping her focus on her task at hand.

"She said she needed my help."

Jordyn gave no response. She wasn't the jealous type, but there was an uneasy feeling in her gut. Something that told her Mega wasn't completely over his relationship with Mila. And that was okay for her, she just hoped he would spare her the heartache before he figured out what he wanted to do.

"Well." She paused before leaving the kitchen to take the food to the table. "I think you should help her. She is the mother of your child and I feel like you would regret not helping if something bad happened."

And just like that, she walked over to the table and took her seat. Mega stood in the doorway of the kitchen for a moment, going back and forth in his head about what he would do. The feeling of MJ squirming around in his arms swayed his decision a great deal, though he was afraid of what he might feel if he decided to rescue Mila from herself once again.

There was also some concern about Jordyn in his gut. She didn't seem to care whether he dealt with Mila or not. He wasn't sure if that was because of MJ, or because she wasn't really into him like she portrayed, and that was something he wanted to get down to the bottom of immediately.

"You think I should help her?" he asked as he took a seat next to her at the table.

Pauline recognized a little hostility in his voice and wondered if she should take her food to her room.

"It's not about what I think, Mega." Jordyn rolled her eyes and reached for the baby.

"Then what is it? You don't seem to care whether I do or not."

She ignored him and focused her attention on feeding MJ.

"Alright." He sighed and proceeded to eat his dinner.

There was an awkward silence around the table for a while. One that Pauline couldn't stand amongst them, so she decided to weigh in on the dilemma.

"Is this about the baby's mother?" she asked.

Neither Mega, nor Jordyn spoke up, leaving her to continue on with her observation.

"If it is, I think you should step in and do what you can. That baby needs the both of you, whether you get along in your personal lives or not."

"And that's exactly what I already told him." Jordyn sassed.

"And how do you feel about that?"

It sounded so simple when Pauline asked the question Mega didn't know how to ask. He was afraid his words wouldn't come out as softly as hers did.

"I don't feel any kind of way about it. I know he has to deal with her either way." She looked at him with a stern look on her face. "As long as he doesn't lie to me about the basis of their dealings I have no reason to be upset."

"That's that then." Pauline clapped her hands and dug back into her plate. "This chicken is good! Almost as good as mine."

"Yeah iight!" Mega laughed, feeling a lightness come around the table. "We gotta have a cook-off one day. See who throws down the best."

"I'm with it."

Once dinner was finished and MJ was passed out in her crib, Mega set up the bathroom for Jordyn to relax in the tub. He laid out the candles, prepared a gourmet fruit tray complete with wine and chocolate,and told her to take her time. He also thanked her for everything she'd been doing for him and MJ. Whether she knew it or not, he appreciated her bringing them together more than anything.

Chapter Nine

"Rise and shine, Paulie D."

Mega knocked on the woman's door long before her alarm sounded and to his surprise, she was already awake. Eager to get back in the game and make some real money, Pauline had stayed up all night thinking of a master-plan.

"I been up all night, youngster. You got my wheels spinning and they wouldn't stop."

"Mind of a true hustler." Mega said, and dapped her up. "Get dressed, we got places to be. I'm gonna go make sure our kids are set for the day and I'll meet you outside."

Jordyn was still asleep, while MJ sat in her highchair eating the breakfast Mega made for her. He made sure he was up before the house so that he could spend some alone time with MJ. It was owed to her after the year Mila spent keeping her in hiding. And owed to him too.

Though he'd never talked about having any kids he knew that he would be a good father. He always told himself that if he did slip up and get someone pregnant, he would make sure he was in his child's life no matter what.

"You had enough?" he asked, lifting MJ from the mess she made in her highchair. "Was it good? I can cook a lil bit, huh?"

Once she noticed that her daddy was throwing away the scraps she didn't eat she started to scream. There was nothing but a few orange peels, a couple of mashed up grapes and small chunks of pancake left over.

"You want more?" He laughed a little as he placed her back in her highchair. "That's all you gotta say, we don't do all that acting out over here."

It wasn't long before Jordyn came running into the kitchen like something happened. She'd been sleeping so good she almost forgot there was even a baby in the house.

"Oh my god." She panted, with her hand over her chest. "I thought she got out of her crib and fell down the stairs or something."

"Nah, she good. I brought her down here earlier and made her some breakfast. You too." He smiled and sat a plate down on the table for her. "Me and Paulie D got a few errands to run, so I wanted to let you rest up before I asked you to babysit."

"Look at daddy being all sweet." She walked over to Mj, who was wailing her arms in the air for Jordyn to pick her up. "He really got up early and made us breakfast. Got you all changed and dressed and everything. Good job, daddy."

Mega stood at the stove observing the way MJ reacted to seeing Jordyn. It was a cute sight to see, he just didn't want her to grow accustomed to thinking that Jordyn was her mother.

In the back of his mind he wondered if their relationship would be the same if he and Jordyn had their own kid. She wasn't the type of chick to change up on the people she cared about, so he was betting nothing would change. It was just something to think about now that he was playing an active role in his daughter's life.

"Where y'all going?"

"To run a few errands."

"Ok, but where? It's not everyday that my mama runs errands with my boyfriend. Shit, I couldn't even get her to sit down for dinner with the last one."

"And I don't blame her." He leaned in and kissed her after checking his phone. "I gotta go. Call me if you need anything."

"Mhm. MJ wants a kiss too, don't be stingy."

Mega did more than just give MJ a kiss. He took his baby girl into his arms and hugged tight. She hugged him back too. Then, after planting what seemed like a thousand kisses on her cheeks and chubby little neck, he handed her back to Jordyn and made his way to the front door.

Jordyn's heart melted at the sight of Mega and his tiny twin. Sometimes she felt a streak of jealousy striking her heart because she also wanted what Mila had with Mega, but her feelings for MJ never changed. She grew to love her more and more as each day passed.

It was a mystery what would happen if Mila returned. That was the only thing Jordyn feared. It would hurt her to not be able to see MJ. Even worse if Mila decided to take her away from Mega too. There were times where she wanted to reach out to her enemy and let her know that her baby was fine and schedule a sit down, but she had reached out enough. She figured when Mila was ready to settle things like grown women, she would pick up the phone and do just that. Until then, Jordyn played her role and kept the kid safe.

"Well dang, good morning to you too ma!" She called out to her mother who was rushing towards the door.

"Oop! I'm sorry." Pauline doubled back to the dining room to greet her daughter, and MJ.

"Good morning to you." She kissed Jordyn's head. "And good morning to you." She did the same to MJ. "I'll see y'all later."

"You and Mega are gonna make me kill y'all." Jordyn laughed. "See you later."

Neither of them told Jordyn where they were going, or what they were going to do, but she had a feeling she already knew. She didn't like what she knew, but Pauline did what she wanted to do anyway, so there was nothing Jordyn could say to stop her.

"Hey Paulie D, can I ask you something?"

Pauline knew from experience that whenever someone started their conversation off like that, the question was about to be serious.

"Yeah, hit me."

"What's up with Charles? Like, I know y'all had it out once upon a time, but that's over now? You're completely done with him? I know how women can be. Y'all hold onto love for a long time. I just don't want nothing coming in between what I got going on."

Charles was a nightmare Pauline wanted to keep buried in her past. But, for the sake of earning Mega's trust, she braced herself before she spoke his name.

"Charles was my first love." She started, with a slight glimmer in her eye. "That love is gone now. Long gone."

"So you wouldn't feel no way if he was taken out?"

Back in the day she might have. Even after he blew her back out with his shotgun she still carried a soft spot in her heart for Charles. It took a long time for her to get over him, but once she was done, that was it.

"Not at all. Especially now that I know he's after my babies."

"Speaking of," Mega interrupted, wanting to get some closure for his best friend. "What's the story with you and Layton? She was really hurt when she found out that he was her dad. I was surprised too. We'd been doing business with the man for years and he never once mentioned having kids."

Another story Pauline dreaded to tell. She wasn't at all proud of the way she handled having her first child. She was, however, happy that things turned out the way they did, instead of the way they would have if she would've stuck around.

"I was too strung out to care for Layton the way she deserved to be cared for. I'm never gonna be proud of that, but I do feel like I made the best decision when it came to her well-being."

"I respect that." Mega nodded. "She turned out alright."

"Yeah, she did." Pauline chuckled lightly. "My best friend did a good job with her."

"The lady Jen you're always talking about? That's Jen who raised Layton?"

"Yep."

Mega knew Jen. Layton had taken him out to Philly to meet her a few times. It was crazy to him that he hadn't put two and two together after hearing Pauline talk about it.

"Damn, that's what's up. That lady is a true rider."

"Oh yeah! That's my girl. She always has my back, no matter what."

The chat with Pauline cleared up a lot of things for Mega. Not that he didn't trust Pauline would be a good business partner, he was just interested in her past. He wanted to know what made her the woman she was. What triggered her. How she handled her money in the drug game. Not just any kind of money, but a lot of money. And most importantly, he wanted to make sure that all of her ties to the Hitman were severed. In case there came a day when he had to X Charles out.

On the way to one of Mega's drop-spots, Jordyn texted him to tell her what she had planned for the day. It wasn't something he required for her to do, but he did like when she did it. Mila never let him know what she was doing at all, until she was already doing it.

"You know you don't have to tell me your every move, right? I trust you." He replied.

"I know I don't, but it makes me feel safe I guess. That way if something happens to me you know where to look first. And not only that, but I do have your kid with me. You need to know where she is at all times."

"I know. I appreciate you for that. For real."

"You're welcome. I appreciate you also, for helping me with my mom and everything."

"Your moms and I are about to do some great business together."

"I figured. And Whatever you two have going on, I don't wanna know nothing about. Just be safe. Please."

"We will. Enjoy your time out. I left you some money on the counter downstairs. Do whatever you want with it, just grab me some Lifesavers before you go home."

Mega was the most thoughtful man Jordyn knew. She still owed Kaylani a grand for the role she played in kidnapping MJ and had no idea how she was going to pay her off, being that she quit her job to be her man's nanny, so whatever money he'd left her came right on time.

"You left five thousand dollars on the counter…." She texted him again, just to be sure she had the right money.

"Yeah…."

"What you mean yeah….? Is this what you left for me!!?"

"Yeah, is that not enough?"

Mega figured since she was the offspring of the Queen of Philly she was used to having wads of cash at her disposal. But, after he thought about it, Pauline was on the decline around the time Jordyn really figured out what having money meant. Things in her adult life were very different.

"More than enough." She replied. "Now I can give Kaylani the rest of her money for helping me. Thank you."

She never did tell Mega the full story of what happened with Kaylani. He didn't ask either. There was a little suspicion lingering around in his head though. As soon as people found out you had money to throw around the game always changed. He just hoped Jordyn knew what she was doing when it came to the ones she played.

"Be careful J. I know that's your friend and you know her better than I do, but keep your eyes open. You never know what people might do when there's money involved."

Jordyn had never had a reason to question Kaylani's loyalty to her, but she knew Mega was right. Shit, her own father tried to kill her mother in front of her over some money. That experience alone kept Jordyn on her toes when it came to more than just money. She was skeptical when it came to life in general.

Chapter Ten

After talking to her man, Jordyn was a little on edge about meeting up with Kaylani. They hadn't talked much since the kidnapping, which was neither a good thing or a bad thing, the vibe was just a little off. Jordyn didn't know whether Mila had gotten to Kaylani and the whole meetup was a set up, or if Kaylani showed up as a friend. Either way, she had her little .22 Mega gave her and was ready to use it if she had to.

Kaylani looked a little nervous when she pulled up to the park they were meeting at. Nothing too out of the ordinary, seeing as though they did commit a crime that could have gotten them both killed.

It didn't take long for her to shake her nerves and calm the tension Jordyn felt in her gut. She knew her girl was as solid as they came. And if someone did happen to get to her, she would've figured out a way to let it be known.

"Look at you playing somebody's mama." Kaylani said, smiling hard as hell when she saw her friend.

"Girl!" Jordyn quickly grabbed her in for a hug. "I'm so happy to see you, oh my god. I just knew this shit was gonna backfire. How you been? I'm sorry it took so long for us to meet up, I just wanted to make sure everybody was safe first."

"Don't sweat it. You my girl and I got you. I told you that."

Jordyn scanned Kaylni's face for sincerity and found exactly what she was looking for. A true and honest friend.

"Here you go," Jordyn said, handing over an envelope full of cash. "I put a lil something extra in there for your troubles."

"Thank ya kindly." Kaylani playfully teased.

She was surprised to see Jordyn with the baby still. She thought Mila would've come and got her, or her dad would have her. It made her a little upset to see, to be honest.

"So, what's going on with this? Why do you still have the baby? Where's her dad?"

"Out running errands with my mama." Jordyn shrugged.

"Okay? Why isn't she with them?"

Jordyn knew how Kaylani felt about her jumping into relationships. She hated Polo and she was sure to hate any other man who entered Jordyn's life. She was so overprotective of her friend sometimes, she forgot that Jordyn was a grown woman and could date whoever she wanted.

"I know what you're getting at Kay," Jordyn rolled her eyes. "Mega isn't like that. He's a really sweet guy and he helps me out a lot. Shit, he's the one who gave me the money to be able to pay you."

"Money ain't shit to a guy like him, Jordyn. Don't let no man buy you out of your dignity. What's gonna happen when the baby-mama comes back? Did you even think about that?"

"Whoa-whoa, buy me out of my dignity? I wouldn't go that far. Mega has been very transparent with me about everything when it comes to him and the baby's mother. So, I don't see him moving funny now."

"Okay." Kaylani threw her hands up in peace. "No need to get feisty with me, I'm just looking out for my friend. This ain't just some nigga who had a kid and moved on. He just found out that he had a kid with this girl, so trust me, they have a lot of shit to talk about that won't involve you."

Those words struck a nerve for Jordyn. Mostly because she knew Kaylani was right. No matter how much she wanted her friends' support in her decision to submit to Mega, Kaylani was right. There were a lot of conversations to be had between him and the mother of his child. Ones that couldn't involve Jordyn until they got things squared away between the two of them first.

"Look, I just don't want you to end up hurt behind this shit. I've seen that too many times. Mega probably is a good dude, but you still gotta protect you. Alright?"

"Alright." Jordyn replied after a moment of silence. "On a different note, what's been up with you? You ain't seen nobody suspicious lingering around have you?"

"Surprisingly, no. I thought for sure baby mama would run up and get her ass beat, or send somebody to do her dirty work for her, but nah. My life has been as quiet as it always is."

"Good." Jordyn laughed. "I really don't want you getting into no shit because of me."

Kaylani really didn't mind the drama Jordyn brought to her life. She felt like she needed the excitement after breaking things off with her long time girlfriend.

"What ever happened to you finding out you had a sister?"

"Oh!" Jordyn quickly remembered. "That's crazy right!? I haven't even sat down and really talked to my mom about what happened yet though. She's already had a hard enough life,

I don't wanna make her sad about that shit on top of everything else we have going on. But, Layton and I are alright. I mean, we haven't sat down and really dug into each other's backgrounds or nothing like that, but she seems cool. A little bitter, maybe, but nothing we can't work on."

"I'm still in shock, honestly. Miss Pauline never talked about having another kid when we were growing up. Never even hinted towards it at all. I'm sure she had a good reason to do what she did, it's just so crazy to me."

"Shit, imagine how I felt when I found out."

Jordyn stared down at MJ playing and cooing in her stroller and wondered what her sister's life was like as a child. She hoped it was good. Layton expressed that it was, but people were known to mask a lot of things to keep people out of their business.

"I think I'm gonna call her and see if she wants to sit down and talk. I've been meaning to, ever since we found out, I guess I just don't know how to bring up the conversation."

"How is she? With everything that happened at the lake house and everything?"

"I'm not sure." Jordyn shrugged, a little embarrassed. "Mega said she was finally home from the hospital, so maybe now is the perfect time to catch her with nothing else better to do."

Kaylani agreed. She and Layton had run into each other a few times around town, so she knew she was cool. She also thought Layton was cute. One of the many reasons she wanted Jordyn to be on a good foot with her. She wanted her girl to put her on.

"Let me know how it goes." Kaylani said, giving Jordyn a look that a fool couldn't miss.

"Oh god," Jordyn laughed and rolled her eyes. "I already know what type of time your ass is on."

"What?" Kaylani laughed like she didn't know what Jordyn was talking about. "I'm just saying. I think it would be good for you to have a sister in your life. Besides me, of course."

"Mhm. I bet. And what would you like me to tell this sister of mine for you? Cause I know that's what you want. You ain't slick."

Jordyn knew her friend like the back of her hand. They'd been inseparable since they were little girls and nothing had ever changed. Every time Kaylani had a crush on somebody she sent Jordyn through as her messenger.

That was something Jordyn never understood, though. Kaylani was a beautiful girl with a dope personality. She was just shy when it came to initiating conversation with someone she was interested in.

"Hold up," Jordyn waved her finger in the air. "What happened to whats-her-name? Aren't y'all still a thing?"

"Ugh." Kaylani rolled her eyes. "Girl, no. I had to get rid of her ass."

"Well damn, you just a playa from the Himalaya's aren't you?"

"I guess you could say that."

One thing about Kaylani, she didn't play with relationships. Her three strike rule was more official than the major leagues. Sometimes she didn't even tell a motherfucker when they got their first strike. Just as soon as they hit their third, the game was over.

"Well what happened with y'all? I kind of liked her. And she was the longest person I ever seen you keep around."

"Right? I liked her too, she just had too much baggage. Talking about she still keeps in contact with her ex because they co-parent. Yeah, okay. Who I look like, boo-boo the fool?"

"Maybe she was telling the truth."

"Nope. I saw as much as I needed to see and sent her right back to the ex. They can co-parent in peace now."

After a long catch and some lunch from one of the local food stands in the park, Jordyn and Kaylani said their goodbyes. It was still early in the day and Jordyn really didn't want to be in the house, but there was nothing for her to do. Especially with a one year old on her hip.

She thought about calling Mega and asking him to hang out with them, but that was out of the question. She knew not to bother him too much while he was handling business.

Then, the idea of calling Layton popped back into her head. After a while of sitting on the park bench watching MJ snack on her ice cream, she decided she might as well call. It was almost time for MJ to be put down for a nap anyway, so Layton's place was a great next stop. Jordyn just didn't know how to bring the conversation about.

"Let's see if she answers." She said to herself, as she pressed the call button on her phone.

It took a few rings, but Layton picked up. She didn't sound too enthused either.

"What's up?" Layton spoke into the receiver.

"Nothing, how are you?"

"I'm good. What you need?"

"I don't need anything. I was calling because I'm in the area and wanted to see if we could sit down and talk."

Layton looked at her phone like it grew legs or something. She understood that Jordyn was her sister and everything, but she wasn't ready for the fairytale family reunion just yet.

"Talk about what? If it's about that lakehouse bullshit, nah. I don't really wanna recap on all that right now."

"Well, good. Because I don't wanna talk about that either. I wanna talk about us. Get to know you a little bit. I mean, we are family. Maybe I can give you some insight on our mother and what life was like for her back then. I don't know." Jordyn shrugged, bashfully

Things went silent for a moment. There were a lot of things Layton wanted to know about her birth mom, she just wasn't sure if she was ready to hear the whole truth so soon.

Then, she thought about it. If Jordyn was going to be someone constant in Mega's life, she had to get to know her. It would've been awkward being around a sister she had no real relationship with. She'd always wished she had a sibling growing up anyway, so she figured maybe that wish had finally come around.

"Yeah, ok. Cool. I'll text you my address. And yo." She said, making sure she had Jordyn's undivided attention. "Make sure don't nobody follow you here. I can't afford to have niggas knowing where I rest my head after everything that went on."

"I got you. I'm on my way."

The conversation went smoother than Jordyn imagined it would. She thought for sure Layton would've told her to fuck off or something, but she was cool.

Chapter Eleven

When Jordyn pulled up to Layton's crib, she wasn't surprised at all by how nice it was. She already knew that if Mega was her best friend, she lived lavishly just like he did. That was something she picked up on the night they met each other at the white ball.

She lived in a bougie ass neighborhood too. Out there with the white folks where the grass was always greener. That alone let Jordyn know what kind of money she was bringing in. Shit, it almost made her want to get in on the game herself.

"Don't even ask." Jordyn immediately lectured when she saw the look on Layton's face as opened the door. "Your friend has me babysitting. I think he's scared of babies or some shit."

Layton laughed at that, because she already knew the situation.

"Well shit, y'all come in. make yourself at home."

Dressed in nothing but a black mink robe and holding a beer in her hand, Layton left Jordyn to lock up while she headed back to the living room. She had no plans on entertaining company that day, so whatever Jordyn had in mind would have to be discussed at her leisure.

"Damn, this is a nice ass crib." Jordyn admired, as she followed her sister's footsteps.

"Yeah, it's a lil something-something."

"More than a lil something."

Layton's place was decked out like one of those homes in the magazines. Hardwood floors. Granite countertops. Nice ass living room set with a cinema sized TV mounted on the wall. Upstairs, downstairs, and even came equipped with a pool. She was definitely doing good for herself.

"So, what's up?" Layton asked. "What brings you out here to see me?"

"Just wanted to chat."

Layton took a good look at Jordyn while she got MJ changed and ready for her nap. She wasn't sure of what she was looking for, it was just weird knowing that she had a sister she knew nothing about.

"If I didn't know any better I would think that's your child."

"Cute, right?" Jordyn laughed a little.

"She is cute. Look just like Mega ass."

Layton felt a bubbly feeling looking at MJ. She and Mila had never seen eye to eye, but that wasn't enough of a reason for Layton to not want to be involved in MJ's life. Besides, she was Mega's daughter too.

"Y'all ain't heard nothing from Mila's ass?"

"Your boy has. She texted him the other night talking about how she needs his help."

"Need his help!? After she just tried to have the man killed? She real funny."

Jordyn agreed, but she thought about MJ before anything. Though she didn't mind playing mommy, she knew MJ needed Mila in her life. If it were her baby she would want someone to think the same way about her.

Once MJ was asleep on her mat, Layton took Jordyn out on her patio so they could have a drink and talk without waking her up. There were a lot of grounds to cover about Layton's childhood and she knew how animated she could get during a serious conversation, so the patio was their best bet. There was no telling what was going to come out of her mouth once the conversation started.

"Look, I'm not really good at starting off conversations, I just cut right to the chase." Layton said. "There's a lot I wanna know about the woman who birthed me. So."

Jordyn respected cutting through the bullshit more than Layton knew. She was the same way.

"Well, ma's not all that bad. She made some fucked up choices, but she isn't a bad woman at all. She was Miss America back in 83, and one of the baddest hustlers in Philly. That's not something I'm always proud to say, but she be happy as hell to tell it."

"Hold up," Layton sat up in her chair. "Ma was a dope girl?"

"Shit, more than that. She had the whole Philly on lock. Anything a motherfucker needed they got it from her."

"Damn. That's what's up"

Layton was already intrigued by what little she heard. It finally made sense as to where she got her hustler mentality from. Her adoptive mom was all about school and keeping a nine-to-five.

"Yeah, it was for a while. Until she met our dad."

"Hitman." Layton spat, ready to put a bullet in his head on sight.

"Yep. When she got with him that's when her life started to fall apart. He was only supposed to be her bodyguard while she was doing her modeling thing, but they ended up messing around and that's when they got pregnant with you. She kept you until you were about three, and when she got hooked on drugs she decided life was too risky to keep you around."

Life was always a risk for Layton. Everyday she walked outside her door. When she drove to work, or to make her drops there was a risk waiting on every corner. So, she had very little sympathy for a mother to not want to take a risk. She guessed she had to look at it another way, though. Had Pauline taken a risk, Layton may not have been alive long enough to listen to her sister tell her story.

"Charles started getting abusive once you were gone and their money stopped coming in as much as it used to. Ma was getting so high she started using her own drugs and ripping off connects and shit. She even lost her modeling contract and every endorsement deal she had."

"That motehrfucker." Layton was so angry with Charles she wanted to hurt somebody. "I can't believe I missed the snake behind his mask."

"Yeah, he was a bad man. When she found out she was pregnant with me she decided it was time to get her life back right. Told

Charles she was leaving him and everything because he didn't wanna get off the drugs."

Jordyn got quiet as the memories from that night vividly flashed in her mind. She hated talking about what Charles did to her mom. She could still smell the blood on her little hands after she tried to put pressure on her mom's wounds, and the gun smoke left lingering in the air. That night, Jordyn thought neither of them would live to see another day.

"You ok?" Layton asked, noticing tears forming in her sister's eyes.

"Yeah." Jordyn took a deep breath and gulped from the glass of wine Layton pushed towards her. "I get the chills thinking about what he did to her. I can still feel the wetness from her blood on my hands when I talk about it."

"What happened?"

"When ma said she was leaving he beat her up pretty bad. She had all of our shit packed and everything. Even after him jumping on her the way he was she still found her strength to leave. When he saw that she was dead asscserious, he ran into their bedroom and grabbed his shotgun."

Complete silence took over the patio. Layton already knew what Jordyn was going to say, but she just had to hear it with her own ears.

The experience wouldn't be as real to her if Jordyn didn't speak it.

"Go on." Layton pushed, with a look of hatred in her eyes. "Tell me what he did to ma."

"He shot her. As soon as she turned to pick me up and run out the door he pulled the trigger!" Jordyn cried. "The sound was so loud I dropped straight to the floor. I was only two years old, I couldn't do anything to help her!" she continued to sob. "It was God's will that she didn't make it to me as fast as she thought she could, cause I might've been dead today."

Layton felt Jordyn's pain like she was there and after downing the last of her beer, she rushed to her sister's side to be the support she needed. The shoulder she needed to cry on after getting that story off her chest. She'd held those tears in for so long, it felt good to get them out. And even better to have someone there to console her while she did it.

"I was smart for a two year old, though." She laughed a little through her tears. "She always taught me that if something happened, or I got a cut or something, to put pressure on it. I don't know how I remembered that shit after seeing what I saw, but I did. So while I'm down on the floor using whatever I could find to cover up the blood, Charles runs out of the house and just leaves me there."

Rage filled Layton's veins as she listened to Jordyn recap the night her mom almost lost her life. She silently swore she would kill Charles herself, no matter who had his head on payroll. Not only for what he did to her mom, but what he did to her as well. And Jordyn.

"How did she walk away from that? Layton asked, still cradling Jordyn in her arms.

"Miss Jen. The lady who adopted you? They've been best friends since grade school. She said she had a feeling in her gut that something wasn't right and God's will she came over to check, because ma wasn't answering her phone."

A chill ran down Layton's spine. Hearing those words made her love her mom ten times more than she already did. She may not have been into the streets like Layton was, but she damn sure was a ride-or-die.

"As soon as she ran up the driveway and heard me crying she burst right through the door. Already had the police on the way to the house and everything. I don't know what it was she felt, but that shit must've been strong as hell, cause she ain't play no games that day."

"Damn right." Layton chimed in.

"Ma is such a strong woman, man. She fought all the way until they got her to the hospital. When she flatlined, Miss Jen was right there telling her to keep fighting. And she never left her side the whole time she was laid up."

"Now that you say that, I do remember her being gone for a while. I thought she got fed up with my dad and decided to leave me with him, but she did say that she was taking care of a friend. Just never said who that friend was."

"Yeah," Jordyn slowly nodded her head. "If it wasn't for her, I don't know where I'd be. Ma had so much pull with the Philly police they made sure I got to stay with Miss Jen at the hospital, instead of being placed in foster care."

Jordyn told Layton everything she needed to hear. She was still a little sad to know that her mother didn't keep her, but she was satisfied with finally knowing why things happened the way they did.

When she texted her mom and told her that she'd finally met Jordyn, the woman was happy for her. It had been a long time coming and had it not been for Pauline wanting to make that reunion happen herself, Jen would've made the first move.

"I'm gonna kill that motherfucker." Layton said, calmly looking out at the water in her backyard.

She was expecting Jordyn to try and talk her out of it or something, but she didn't. She agreed that it was something that needed to be done, before he got to one of them. There were plenty of nights she stayed up plotting on how she would take him out herself, she just never knew where to find him.

"I wanna be there when you do."

Chapter Twelve

Mega had a few different stash houses throughout the lower half of Florida. He had some crazy ass, hardcore ass niggas running them too. The one he decided to take Pauline to was ducked off in a small town called Immokalee. Where all the chico's reside. That was his personal favorite. He felt at home down there. They also had great food and a casino that wasn't as ghetto as the ones in Miami.

He figured that if Pauline was going to be put on payroll, he would let her set up shop somewhere around Immokalee. There wasn't too much traffic and being that she was an old-timer, that'd be one of the safer places for her to be. Of course, he would have niggas watching her back, but the less traffic - the better.

"Alright Og." Mega said, as he parked his jeep. "Let's see what you know."

Pauline took a good look at the house they were parked in front of. She already knew it was a stash house, because why else would she have to show him what she knew about a house?

"It's definitely one of your spots."

Mega nodded his head and waited for her to state what else she noticed.

"All work. No money is kept here. Not a large amount anyway. I know that because I didn't see too many banks in the area." She went on. "I'd say there's probably three to four women inside. One man. House looks real tidy and kept up. Men don't care about that kind of shit. Three rooms and a bunker. Judging from the looks of this town I'd say there's probably a little old Spanish woman who comes through and cooks some good food too."

He laughed and nodded his head, a little shocked that she was able to call out his entire spot. The only motherfuckers who could read a dope house as well as she did, was a hustler. Not just any hustler, but a BIG TIMER.

"Hit the nail right on the head, old timer. Get out and let's go inside. Shit, this place could be yours someday."

The moment they stepped inside, everything Pauline spoke of was right there in her face. Everything from the one man holding down the front door, down to the old Spanish woman cooking up a hot meal in the kitchen. Mega's special request.

"Wow." Pauline's eyes widened at all the product she saw lying around. "I ain't seen this much dope since the 80's."

Mega worried about whether she would get that itch to start using once she laid eyes on what he was holding. He wanted to ask her about it, but didn't want to tempt her. Or be disrespectful.

"You think you can handle something like this if the time comes?"

"If it's anything like what I'm used to, hell yeah."

There were drugs everywhere inside the house. Packaged up on the couches. All over the tables. In the garage. On the floor. Inside the walls. If there was a place that could hold it, there were drugs in it or on it. Pauline felt like it was a little risky, but everybody had their own escape plan laid out too. If the police ever raided the spot there was a tunnel underneath the floorboards with four pathways dug out.

Each way led to a different destination. And each destination had a designated driver ready for a pick-up just in case they got that call.

"Everybody keeps their mouths shut. I like that." Pauline pointed out the silence she heard during her tour of the place.

"Yeah. Ain't nobody friendly around these parts unless I give the word. I can't have no chatterboxes running my operation. That's the quickest way to sink the ship."

"You preaching to the choir, young blood."

After giving Paulie D the rundown of the place, Mega sat her down in the bunker to give her more details. He told her exactly how he ran his business, when it came to getting rid of the dope and storing the money. Dope went one way, money went another. He learned his lesson about keeping them both in the same location, so if the cops came and kicked the door in it was either one or the other. He wasn't willing to give up both.

"How much money you think is in here?" he asked, trying to get a feel for Pauline's eyesight.

"Too much, if I'm being honest."

Right away he knew the woman knew her product. He was getting ready for a shipment later that night, otherwise there wouldn't have been so much shit lying around.

"I'd say two mill. Easy."

"Right on." He nodded and leaned back in his chair. "We got a drop later tonight to get rid of some of this shit. You definitely right though, there's too much. I usually don't keep this much in one spot, but some niggas didn't have their money up so I had to hold on to it."

"What's your way of distribution?" she asked, wanting to know if the game had changed from back in her day.

"Depends." He shrugged. "If I'm supplying in the states it's usually a drop-off and pick-up by one of my runners. If it's something overseas it hits the water or the air. I got a few people on my team for that."

Sounded a lot like the way Pauline did business back in the day. She wasn't as hands on as Mega was, because she was a beauty queen, but if she did ever have to get her hands dirty that wasn't a problem either.

In the midst of giving Pauline the full rundown, Mila called. She had called a few times that morning, but Mega didn't pick up. He wasn't sure of how to conversate with her after everything that happened. Truth be told, he was afraid of what he might start to feel for her once again.

After the tenth time she called, he got a funny feeling and decided to step away from Pauline to call her back.

"Im'a step out and make a phone call real quick. I'll have Santoya bring you in some grub. Trust me, it's fire."

"I can tell by the way it smells. And take your time, I got a call to make myself."

Mega sat in his jeep with the air running while he made his call. It took him a minute to build up the nerve to press dial, but he got over it quickly because he knew they had to talk sooner or later.

"What's up?"

"Yo." She paused to catch her breath. "Thanks for calling me back. I know I'm the last person you ever wanted to hear from."

There was a silence between them. Neither of them were sure of what to say to the other, even though there was a lot to be said.

"How's MJ?"

A softness washed over him when she spoke their daughter's name. All he could picture in his mind was the three of them together. Like a family.

"She's fine. Got a lot of hair. Just like you." He smiled, looking at the picture Jordyn printed of them together.

"I'm sorry you had to find out about her the way you did. I just," she sighed. "I didn't know how to even tell you. I was ashamed at first because I didn't know whose she was. But, once she started getting bigger I knew she was yours. And I knew you would cuss me out for not telling you. Honestly, I wasn't expecting you to keep talking to me once you found out about Polo."

"I should've stopped." He said, coldly.

"You're not super innocent here, Mega. Don't act like you wasn't doing your dirt."

"Is that what you called me to talk about? Cause if so, I don't have time for this."

Her ego wanted to go off on him, but she knew she deserved whatever he threw at her. She crossed a line that wasn't going to be easy to recross. It was a wonder he was even still willing to talk to her.

"Look Mega, I know what I did was fucked up. For what it's worth, I knew Polo wouldn't be able to get the job done. I used him to get the money I needed to move away and start a new life for me and my daughter. As far as I knew, when you brought another bitch with you to the ball, we were done. I was gonna use that money to take my baby and disappear. And I knew Polo would try to follow me or some shit, so I had to do something to get him out of my way. I just wanted to be done with this shit and move on with my life."

Every word he feared Mila would say, she said. He knew there was some other reason for her actions. There was no way she really wanted him dead.

"You could've told me all of this. I would've handled that nigga for you and gave you whatever you felt you needed to move on."

"You would've let me take our baby and dip?"

"I didn't even know we had a baby."

Mila knew as soon as Mega found out they had a child her move wouldn't be easy at all. He would've fought her tooth and nail, or they would've had to make things right between them. She guessed she just let her emotions get the best of her and reacted too soon.

That was her problem. When she felt like someone was trying to get over on her, she always made the first move.

"Well, now you do."

A single tear fell from her eye while she waited for him to reply. Mega felt like he was in the twilight zone talking to her. His heart and mind were at war with each other, but most of all he didn't trust her anymore. It was hard for him to. Even though he felt like her explanation was the truth.

"I really need your help, Meg. After what I did I wouldn't be asking if I had a plan to get out of this."

"You know the man you got that money from ain't gonna just accept a payoff. Even if I tripled it, that still wouldn't be good enough. Fuck Mila!" He slammed his fist down on the steering wheel.

"I know." She started to sob. "I fucked up bad."

"Where are you?"

She paused again, not wanting to disclose her location over the phone. She wasn't sure if their phones were tapped, or if someone close by was listening in. She wasn't even sure she could trust Mega 100%. There were all kinds of scenarios running through her head, but with no other options coming to mind she told him where only he would know to find her.

"I'm where the heart meets the mind."

"I'll call you back later. I'm sending somebody to be your lookout, and don't worry about who it is. I trust him."

After ending their call he sat in silence for a moment going over their conversation. Hearing her voice was too surreal for him. He hated how she could do something so fucked up, and then walk right back into his life like nothing ever happened. Worst of all, he didn't want to hurt Jordyn.

"Hey you." A cheery voice spoke into his ear.

"I just talked to Mila." He said without warning. "She wants to meet."

Jordyn's heart sank in her chest. She knew the day would come, she just didn't think she would feel the way she felt about it. However, she was still supportive of their meeting.

"When are you leaving?"

"I don't wanna leave." He said, like an angered child.

"Mega." She spoke softly with a subtle smile on her face. "You should go. Think about MJ."

"Come with me then."

"How is that gonna work? I don't wanna get in between y'all parenting. You know there are things you two need to talk about that don't concern me, right?"

He knew she was right. He figured having her there would make it easier for him to fight his temptation, but she was right. He and Mila did have a lot of things to talk about that Jordyn couldn't be there to hold his hand for.

"You'll be ok." She reminded him. "We'll talk about it more when you get home. We miss you."

Chapter Thirteen

After Jordyn left Layton's place there was nothing but silence to wallow in. She Facetimed her mom and dad for a while, just to fill them in on what she learned about her life and to ask a few questions. But, once that was over there was that silence again. She drank so much beer and wine that she wasn't even getting drunk anymore. After that, she turned her fate towards the pain meds her doctors gave her.

"I can't believe this shit." She laughed into the silence. "My entire life has basically been a lie. Shit, I can't even say I truly know who I am. Can I?"

A question that went unanswered because there was no one there to answer it. She felt alone a lot. Sometimes she loved it, and sometimes it was unbearable. The thought of moving back home to Philly crossed her mind most days, but there was nothing but hatred there for her. The niggas on the block hated the fact that she was getting money and pussy so much, they did some unspeakable things to her one night. Things that not even Mega knew about.

"Hey, just calling to let you know me and MJ made it home safe. I know that was a lot of information to take in earlier, so feel free to call me if you need to talk. Alright, later."

Jordyn had a strange feeling after leaving Layton that day. Something about it just kept nagging her. The look in Layton's eyes when she said she wanted to go after Charles told Jordyn that she was dead serious. It needed to be done, but Jordyn didn't want her to go at that task alone.

She called her sister's phone a few more times that evening, and still no answer. So, after getting MJ washed, fed and in bed, she called Kaylani to ask for a favor.

"What's up, J?"

"Hey, Kay. I need a favor."

"Okay. I got you. What you need?"

"If you're not busy tonight I need you to go over and check on Layton. I'm worried about her."

Kaylani felt like she hit the jackpot. For as long as she had been waiting to bump into Layton again, getting that address was more like a favor for her instead of the other way around.

"I'll head over there now. I'm actually just getting off work."

"Okay, cool. Let me know how she is. I told her about mom today and the look in her eyes afterwards," she shivered. "I don't know. It just gave me the chills."

"Okay. I got you. I'll make sure she's alright."

Once Kaylani was on her way over to Layton's, Jordyn texted her to let her know she was sending her friend to check on her. Just so she didn't get spooked and think anyone was coming to murder her. She figured Layton would be pissed at her for giving out her address, but Jordyn was worried about her. And the way Layton was drinking and popping pills, she had every reason to be.

Before heading to Layton's, Kaylani stopped at home to freshen up. She just knew they were going to hit it off. They had to. She had the biggest crush on Layton for the longest time, and the way Layton looked at her the first few times they saw each other? Told her that she had to be feeling her too. She would be after she showed up wearing no panties, anyway.

Layton checked her phone after a while and saw all of Jordyn's missed calls. When she checked her text messages and saw that she was sending someone to her house, she almost called her back to ask what the fuck, but decided to wait until she saw who it was. She wanted some company anyway, and secretly hoped Jordyn was sending some fine ass shorty to be just that.

An hour passed before Kaylani got there. Layton had been back and forth to the window fifty times wondering when whoever was coming would pull up. When she finally saw the headlights coming up her driveway, her adrenaline started to pump. Along with a beer, she also had her gun in hand while she waited to hear the ring of her doorbell. Just in case it wasn't the person Jordyn had sent.

When she saw Kaylani get out of her car and walk her fine ass towards the front door, she quickly ditched her gun, fixed her robe and sprayed a few squirts of cologne on her neck before she made it to the doorbell.

"Hey." Kaylani smiled. "I'm Kaylani. Jordyn."

"Yeah," Layton interrupted. "She told me she was sending someone over."

"Soooo, you're okay? Didn't drink yourself to death like she thought you did?" she laughed.

"Nah." Layton licked her lips as she sized up her guest. "I'm fine. You wanna come in and double check for a body?"

Kaylani looked her up and down before she stepped inside, and Layton was just as fine as she was the first couple of times they saw each other. Once she got a whiff of the Clive Christian's cologne she was wearing, she became even sexier.

"Nice place." Kaylani complimented as she walked ahead of Layton, swaying her hips.

The seduction in her voice made Layton's knees weak. She thought about texting Jordyn back to thank her for sending such a beautiful gift, but decided to wait until she knew for sure she would be able to unwrap it.

"You like it?" she asked, biting her bottom lip a little.

"Love it." Kaylani turned around to face her. "Wanna show me around?"

Layton wanted to do more than just show her around. She wanted to throw Kaylani's ass down on the couch and plant wet kisses all over her body. And Kaylani would have taken that over the tour any day, little did she know.

After some half-assed tour of her crib, Layton took her houseguest into the kitchen's bar area and fixed her a drink. She figured a drink and a little small talk would help get both of their juices flowing, even though she could tell what Kaylani had in mind already.

Layton saw that she wasn't wearing any panties when she crossed her legs in her chair too. Kaylani lifted her leg just high enough for her to get a glimpse at the lips hidden underneath her skirt. It was a sexy sight for Layton's eyes and also a huge turn-on for her hormones.

"So?" Kaylani asked, after taking a sip of the drink Layton made for her.

"So what?"

"What's eating you? Why does your sister feel like you need a babysitter?"

"Oh!" Layton laughed. "Is that what you are?"

"I can be."

The way Kaylani answered and teased her more and more only intensified the already overflowing sexual tension between them. Layton thought she had been in love before, but after meeting Kaylani, she knew for sure that shit had to have been fake. She felt like she'd experienced love at first sight the moment Kaylani walked through her door.

"I don't know," Layton sighed. "We had a real deep conversation earlier."

"About what?"

With Layton, conversation flowed so smoothly for Kaylani. She wasn't nervous, or shy to ask what she wanted to know. It seemed like Layton already had a softness for her, so her straight-forwardness didn't rub her the wrong way at all. She enjoyed it. It was actually what Layton felt like she craved from a woman.

"Our mom and my childhood." Layton said, amazed at how easy it was for her to open up. "You know my mom? Well, Jordyn's mom?"

"I do." Kaylani nodded. "And it's okay to call her your mom, you know. I mean, she may not have raised you, but she definitely brought you into this world. And Miss Pauline wasn't a bad woman either. She still isn't."

"I heard."

There was a sense of calmness in the air. That loneliness Layton felt earlier was long gone, and she was even smiling and laughing more. Kaylani made her feel a lot lighter about the situation and she appreciated that.

Layton also took Kaylani's mind off of being somewhat of a kidnapper. She never told Jordyn that what they did made her feel terrible inside, but she was able to get it off her chest while talking to Layton.

"You don't plan on kidnapping anymore kids do you?" Layton joked.

"Oh my god! Shut up!" Kaylani laughed and playfully slapped Layton's knee. "I didn't plan on doing it when I did it. But, my girl needed my help, so I did what I had to do."

"I like that. That's what's up. You a true rider."

"Yeah." Kaylani humbly nodded. "I guess I am."

Before either of them knew it, Layton leaned in and kissed her. It was one of the sweetest, most sincere kisses Kaylani had ever felt. She kept her eyes closed while she savored the softness of her lips and the coolness of her breath. Even though Layton had been drinking all day. The sensation sent a chill down her spine so sharp, the goosebumps presented themselves all over her arms and thighs.

"You cold?" Layton asked, still leaning in close to her lips.

Instead of verbalizing her answer, Kaylani shook her and nibbled her own bottom lip a little. Then, she grabbed the collar of Layton's robe and pulled her in for more of what they both wanted.

Things quickly spiced up between them once Layon opened her robe. Her body was as solid as a rock, glistening under the dimness of the lights in the kitchen. When she shook her dreads free of their holder, Kaylani almost melted in her seat.

"Let's go upstairs." Layton said, holding out her hand to the damsel stuck in awe.

"What's upstairs?" Kaylani asked, seduction filling her gaze.

"Come find out."

Layton dropped her robe at the foot of the stairs. She was wearing nothing more than an expensive pair of boxer-briefs and a sports bra, but Kaylani felt like she was draped in the finest of diamonds and gold. The toned-ness of her back, arms, and thighs made Kaylani's nani even more moist than it already was. She was ready for Layton to put it down right then and there, but composed herself enough to walk the stairway to what she was sure to be heaven.

"Hold up. You ain't got no man or nothing like that, do you?"

For a moment, Kaylani thought about replying with something smart, but she was too turned on to waste another second of their time. She already knew the reason Layton had asked anyway. There were a lot of bitches who were bored in their relationships with men, so they stepped outside and had their fun with a woman. And in return, the nigga always found some way to have beef with the stud.

It was a dangerous game that women played way too often. A game that Kaylani had never even thought about taking part in. She'd been attracted to women all her life and no nigga could ever change that.

"I'm not interested in niggas." Kaylani said, as she stepped in closer to Layton. "Never have been. Never will be. And as long as I've been checking you out, you don't have anything to worry about. At least, not when it comes to a nigga." She smiled and ran a finger down Layton's abs. "Now take me upstairs and show me what you have to show me."

Chapter Fourteen

After talking to Mila, the rest of the day wasn't the same for Mega. Pauline knew something was off after his phone call at the spot, but she didn't press him for any information. She understood that everyone had their own private lives and not everything was peaches and cream all the time. As long as he showed her what she needed to know about making that money, she was cool.

The thing was, he didn't trust Mila. She sounded sincere as hell over the phone, but he still couldn't be sure. If anybody else had played him the way she had they would've been in a bodybag a long time ago. He couldn't understand why she was so different. Yeah they had history, but that was what made what she did even more unforgivable. He would've never crossed that line with her, no matter what his reasons were. Unless, he truly had a reason to.

"Eventful day, young blood." Pauline yawned as they finally made their way into the front door. "This old lady is going to shower and rest her bones."

"You good? You want something to eat or anything?"

"Oh nooo," she shook her head and rubbed her belly. "Santoya's good cooking still has me stuffed. I got my lil leftover box, so I'll eat that if I wake up hungry."

"Alright. Goodnight."

While Pauline headed to bed, Mega headed towards the kitchen to fix himself a drink. He immediately wanted to go upstairs and lay up under Jordyn, but he didn't want to bring the energy he felt with him at the time. He had to shake whatever it was he was feeling for Mila off before retreating to Jordyn, because it just wasn't fair to her.

The only other person he knew to talk to was Layton. It was kind of late, but he figured she would be up. Since she had nothing else better to do, except heal. So, that was who he called to release his frustrations.

"What's up? You good?" She asked, as soon as she answered her phone.

"Nigga, yeah I'm good. And what you was gon be able to do if I wasn't?"

He realized his reply was kind of snappy and quickly apologized.

"My bad man," he sighed. "I'm just in a fucked up mood right now."

After the meet and greet Layton had with Kaylani she was in a much better mood, so she didn't even take offense to the way he sounded.

"What happened? Something went bad with the Geechi?"

"Nah. That went smooth. Dude was actually cool as hell, and that bag even weighed extra. It's this shit with Mila. She called me today."

Layton rolled her eyes so hard she almost gave herself a headache. She knew sooner or later Mega would fall right back into Mila's web. He always did and them having a kid only made that shit worse.

"You gon get her out the jam. I already know you."

"That's the thing!" he huffed and puffed as he got up from his seat at the island. "I feel bad for even considering not doing it. I know Mila didn't really mean to do what she did."

"But she did it, Mega!" Layton cut him off. "Shit, imagine if her lil plan actually worked. Then what? I would've had to go find the bitch myself and then she'd be dead anyway."

What Layton said made a ton of sense, but there was still that softness in his heart for her. It got softer when he talked about their daughter and what her future could be like.

Layton understood where he was coming from there, but her trust in Mila was completely different from his.

"Look, whatever you decide to do I'ma support it either way. It don't matter what I say, or what nobody has to say. You do what you feel is right in your heart, alright?"

He took a moment to really hear the wisdom of his best friend. The fact that she hated Mila, but still supported him made him smile a little. He didn't feel as bad as he did for wanting to help after that.

"Thanks, Lay. you always got my back. How you holding up over there anyway? You ain't going crazy sitting in the house all day?"

"Shit, nigga I was! Until Jordyn and the baby came to see me."

"Oh word? They stopped by?" he asked, smiling even harder at the thought of Jordyn lugging his baby around everywhere she went.

"Yeah they did. That lil chunky baby so cute, dawg. Her ass look just like you too."

The happiness in his heart shined through in his voice when he replied. Layton almost thought he was crying when she heard his voice crack, until she realized he was only laughing.

"Jordyn a real one, man. For real. That girl is as solid as they come." Layton said, hoping to give him a little more insight on how to handle things with Mila. "She came through to tell me all about my birth mom and shit. Gave it to me bloodraw. She even cried while she was telling me about the shit Charles did to her. That shit hurt my heart so bad man."

Mega knew a little of what happened between Charles and Pauline, but Jordyn hadn't really confided in him enough to cry about it. That made him feel a little selfish because she was always so focused on everybody else and helping them cope, she never had time to do her own coping.

"And get this," Layton continued. "She even sent a friend over here to give me a happy ending."

"Oh so she a pimp too!?"

"Shit, I guess so!" Layton laughed. "She kept calling to check on me and shit once her and the baby made it home, but I was in here drinking and doing my lil shit, so I didn't answer. Next thing I know I see some bad ass shorty walking up the driveway. Some chick named Kaylani."

"Oh yeah. That's her lil homegirl. The one who helped her do that shit at the daycare."

"Yeah, well she my lil homegirl now too."

Mega laughed while Layton gave him all the juicy details, though he was more focused on how down for everybody Jordyn was. Especially MJ. She was the real wifey-type for real, and he didn't want to lose that. Or worse, make her lose that. Not behind him and his bullshit with Mila.

"Speak of the devil." He smiled when she came walking into the kitchen. "Alright Lay, let me hit you tomorrow. I'ma kick it with her for the night."

"Mhm." Jordyn said, as she pranced over to the fridge. "You sure that's Layton, and not one of your lil hoes."

To throw some water on her fire, Mega put his phone on loudspeaker so she could hear for herself that it was Layton. The last thing she had to worry about with him was a hoe.

"Tell her goodnight." He cheesed.

"Goodnight, Layton." Jordyn called out, just to be sure.

"Ay sis! Thanks for that lil gift you sent."

"Oh lord." Jordyn laughed, already knowing her best friend put it down. "You're welcome. Don't hurt my friend."

"Never that. Alright though, I'll fuck with y'all later."

Immediately after ending the call, Mega got up to hug Jordyn. She was a little surprised to see him being all affectionate, but she soaked it up anyway.

"You okay?" she asked, caressing his back while they hugged.

"Yeah."

"Good."

Their hug lasted a minute longer. Truth be told, Jordyn didn't want it to end. She felt like she had been needing a hug like that for a while and everyone around her had failed to see it.

"Where's MJ?"

"In bed where she's supposed to be at this time. Where I'm about to be in a second. I am tired. Shit, I didn't know having a baby was this much work."

"I'm sorry about having you take care of her all day." He laughed a little.

"It's okay. That's my lil road-dawg."

"I heard!"

He couldn't help but peep how sexy she looked in her PJ's. They weren't even skimpy PJ's, it was just her vibe and comfort around him. He felt like they were truly a couple and had been for some time. His mouth watered a little when he thought about what she looked like without them. And even more when he thought about her carrying his baby. Not just MJ, but one of their own.

"Don't look at me like that." She blushed and took a sip of her orange juice.

"Like what?" he asked, licking his lips. "I'm just looking."

"Mhm. Well, can you come upstairs and take a shower so we can go to bed? I haven't seen you all day. And don't come up here being loud either, I don't want MJ to wake up."

"Yes ma'am." He said, downing the rest of his drink. "I'm coming right now."

She waited at the stairs for him to finish up in the kitchen, just so he could watch her walk up from behind. Jordyn realized that she really hadn't been showing him any intimate love, and he didn't pressure her for it either. If he was anything like Polo, he would've been talking shit to her about them not having sex or creeping around with some hoes. She loved the fact that she didn't have to worry about any of that with Mega. It made her feel the need to give him something special.

"You had to hold my hand to walk up the stairs or something?" he asked, wondering why she was still there.

She shook her head and smiled as she seductively started to walk up. It didn't take him long to catch her drift and when he did, he instantly rocked up in his jeans. Intimacy with

Jordyn was different for him. It wasn't as frequent as he was used to, and that was what he liked about it.

Whenever they did have sex it always felt new, or adeventours, or something. He couldn't really explain the feeling he got from her when it came down to it, he just knew it was the bomb.

She got the shower ready for him while he hit his blunt and got undressed. The sight of him removing his clothes was so taunting, it made her do the same. It wasn't even about the sex for her, but more so the intimacy. She wanted to be close to him. To feel his warmth on her skin. Most of all, she wanted him to love her the same way she loved him.

Already naked and waiting up under the waterfall shower head, she held the door open for him to step inside.

"I missed you today." He said, stepping in close to her. "More than usual."

"I missed you too." She smiled softly.

For a moment they just stood there, holding each other and enjoying the mist that sprayed their bodies. It didn't take long for Mega's manhood to rise to the occasion and interrupt their bonding, though. Jordyn was fine with that. She had been fiending for him all day long anyway.

The feeling of her wet skin brushing up against his chest felt like silk. It made his skin sparkle with goosebumps. It also made him feel all warm and fuzzy inside. A feeling he'd only ever felt for one person before.

"You caressing me like you love me or something." She said, loving the way his hands felt washing all over her curves.

"Is that okay for you?"

She really wasn't sure. She wanted it to be okay, until she heard Kaylani's words replaying in her head. She really didn't want to be hurt by Mega, but she couldn't help herself.

Chapter Fifteen

"Charles." Bossy tried his best to keep his composure when he called the Hitman's phone. "Have you laid eyes on our girl? It's been nearly a week and I haven't heard a single word from you since."

Charles wanted to throw his phone into a wall the second he heard it ring. Or better, Bossy's face.

"New York is a big city." Charles said, gritting his teeth. "I need more time to locate her, but don't worry. I have someone on her side working with me." He lied.

"Oh, I'm not worried." Bossy squealed. "I'm never worried. It is you who should be worried. You have seventy-two hours to locate the girl and get me my meeting, or you won't have to worry about anything else ever again."

After Bossy hung up in his ear, Charles let out a loud roar from his gut. He wanted to kill Bossy, and everyone else he had working for him. He hated being some kind of do-boy to such a prissy, temper-tantrum throwing, brat.

"I'm gonna kill that motherfucker!" Charles growled into the noisy streets of New York.

The people walking the sidewalks looked at him like he was some kind of madman at first, but then again it was New York City. There were madmen everywhere.

When he got into his car he sat behind the wheel for a moment, pounding his fist into his hand. That was one of the many ways Charles had learned to cope with his anger. Causing pain was the only thing that helped him steer clear of turning back to drugs those days.

Sometimes, when he thought back on what his life had become, he hated himself. Especially for the way he treated Pauline. He told himself all the time that if he could go back in time and do things differently, he would. No questions asked.

"Alright Charles." He did his best to calm himself. "You're one of the best trackers in the world, you can find this bitch. Just get your head together."

While he waited for anything interesting to happen, he thought about what he wanted to do to Bossy. Most of all, he had to figure out a way to get himself out from under his grip. Charles knew that Bossy was planning to have him killed whether he found Mila or not, and he wasn't about to go down without a fight.

He'd made a lot of enemies over the years, thanks to his drug addiction, so there weren't many people he could call and ask for help. His only option was Mila. he figured that if he could somehow get her to work with him, he might've been able to spare both of their lives. The thing was, nobody knew where to find her. Not even her own mother.

"Hey, it's investigator Larkins again. Just calling to see if you've heard anything from your daughter. My team really needs to speak with her."

Before leaving for New York, Charles had tracked down Mila's mom and fed her some fake story about him being a private investigator. He hoped the woman would start talking if she felt like Mila was in some kind of trouble, but she wouldn't budge. That was how he felt, anyway.

Brenda really didn't know where Mila was and even if she did, she wouldn't tell the police. She didn't care how much trouble they said she was in. She would never turn on her daughter.

"Investigator Charles, how are you? Unfortunately I haven't heard anything about hers, or my granddaughters, whereabouts. I really wish someone would tell me something so that I can stop worrying myself to death." She halfway lied. "Have you been able to at least locate the city she's in?"

Charles felt like the woman was lying, but he had no solid proof. Shit, he wasn't even the real police. She wasn't obligated to tell him anything anyway.

"Well, has she called you any? Maybe you can give me her phone number so I can try and reach out. It's best if she speaks with me about the incident we're investigating before the hole gets any deeper. You said she has a daughter, right? I'd hate to see her get into any trouble and be taken away from that."

Brenda knew all too well about the lengths the police would go to get the information they wanted. And she wasn't budging. Not even at the mention of Mila being taken away from MJ. If there was going to be any information given out, it would have had to come from Mila herself, because Brenda's lips were sealed.

"I'm sorry." She sighed. "I haven't heard anything. She knows not to call me because I'll be the first person to try and talk her down from whatever it is she's got going on. I don't mean to cause you any trouble with your investigation Mr. Larkins, but Mila is still my child. I don't want her getting hurt, or causing her any trouble that doesn't need to be caused. If she calls me I'll let her know you need to speak with her and give her your information. If that's okay with you?"

It didn't matter if it was okay with Charles or not, she wasn't giving him anything more than that.

"Yes ma'am. I understand. But, be very sure to let her know that I won't stop looking until my investigation is complete. Enjoy the rest of your day."

Charles tossed his phone down onto the passenger seat and let his head fall back onto his headrest. He was frustrated with looking for Mila. It was like she just vanished into thin air. There wasn't a single trace of her, other than her ticket purchase to New York. And even that could've been a detour.

With no leads in the city, Charles decided to head over to Philadelphia. His old stomping grounds. He figured that if he was going to be dead soon, he may as well go back home and enjoy what little time he had left in his life. He had no family or anyone special waiting for him. He just wanted to see what his city was like one last time, before he eventually took his last.

A lot of things had changed, but everything was still the same. The food stands on the streets. The addicts and dealers on every corner. The kids running and playing ball on the sidewalks. A smile crossed his face when he thought back to his own kids. He wished he wasn't so fucked in the head back then to have enjoyed their company more.

As he cruised the streets taking in the scenery of his old neighborhood, his head nearly spun a 360. He spotted her. Long, dark, curly haired Mila. walking the streets of Philadelphia like she owned the place. He thought about hopping the curb and testing his speed at grabbing her, but knew his old age had slowed him down a great deal. So, he followed her.

She walked about ten blocks before she finally cut into an alleyway. One that Charles was very familiar with. He remembered there being a small hotel at the top of an old Chinese Buffet, and that was exactly where Mila had gone. Unless she went into the alley to shoot up and to Charles, that didn't look like something she was into.

He waited about twenty minutes before getting out of his car to cross the street towards the alleyway. Just in case she left suddenly, or had someone else meeting her there. Charles wasn't as young as he once was, so a fight wasn't something he was looking to get into. He also didn't want to just run into the building slinging his gun around. In his experience, that was never good for business.

There were only fifteen rooms present on top of the buffet and only a few of them were occupied. Charles took cover in the doorway of the stairwell to listen for any familiar voice, instead of asking the first person he saw if they had seen her. He didn't want anyone in his business, or to be able to point him out to the police if anything happened.

It was getting dark outside before he finally heard any noise. The sound of a phone ringing came from one of the middle rooms in the building and the second he heard it, he rushed out of his hiding spot to listen in for the voice.

The voice was muffled between the door and the hallway of course, but it was just loud enough for Charles to be able to recognize. He thought about kicking the door in and snatching her up, but that would make too much noise. Besides, he wasn't out to kill her anymore. He wanted to come up with a plan. For both of them.

He waited a while before he finally caught up with one of the maids of the place. He pretended to be locked out of his room and since it was just a hole-in-the-wall hotel, the woman let him in. She figured, a well-dressed man like

Charles had no reason to lie about being locked out of some shitty hotel room in the trenches of Philly. Hell, people barely even wanted to stay there.

Mila was in the shower when he entered the room. Great for him, but for sure to be a shock to her. He looked through a couple of her bags and tried to get into her phone while he waited, but had no luck. It was locked. Once he heard the water shutting off he quickly hid at the entrance of the door and waited for her to come out of the bathroom. And once she did, they both got the shock of their lives.

"What the fuck are you doing in my room!? Who are you!?" she shouted, pointing a gun at him. "Who are you!?"

"Calm down!" Charles said, with both of his hands in the air. "I'm here to help you."

"Bullshit!"

She thought he might've been whoever Mega said he was going to have watching out for her, but knew that wasn't possible. She left the location she told Mega she would be because she got scared. She thought he was sending someone to kill her.

"My name is Charles. I know Mega and Layton. I swear, I'm only here to help you."

"Neither of them know where I am, so try again." She said, aiming the gun higher towards the middle of his head. "If you don't start telling some motherfucking truth in this bitch, you won't walk out of here alive. I promise you."

Charles felt a chill come over him. Mila was dead serious. She reminded him a little bit of Jackie Brown in her prime, and he wasn't ready to test his luck.

"Okay, okay!" He continued to plead for her to lower her gun. "I work for Bossy."

The sound of his name nearly sent Mila into a panic. She knew it wouldn't be too long before he finally caught up to her.

"Now listen, he sent me here to round you up as collateral."

"Collateral?"

"He wants Mega to work for him and figures that if he has you, he'll agree to do some business for him. It's either that, or he kills all of our ass. Me for sure."

"And why should I give a fuck about you?" she scoffed. "I could kill you right now and save him the trouble."

"Yeah, you could do that." Charles finally dropped his hands, knowing that she wouldn't pull the trigger. "But, that won't get you off the hook any more than you already are. He'll just send someone else after you. Your mom. Your daughter."

Her heart shattered when he mentioned her daughter. Mila would kill herself if anything ever happened to MJ.

"Now look, I think I have a way to save us both. Mega, I'm not too sure about. He wants me dead anyway."

Mila's ears were open to hearing what Charles had to say, only if it made sense. She didn't want Mega getting killed if Bossy were just going to kill them all anyway. It wasn't worth it to her.

"What's the plan?"

Chapter Sixteen

Mega got up early the next morning so that he could be on time to make his drop and get back to the shop to take care of his client. He was starting some badass leg sleeve that afternoon and wanted to give himself the time to finish up early enough to get back home to Jordyn. The way she put it on him in the shower the night before had him not even wanting to get up and go to work.

"What you got planned for the day?" he asked, calling her as soon as he pulled out of the driveway.

"I haven't even gotten out of bed yet." She giggled. "I don't know. Probably go hang out with Kaylani. She texted me last night wanting to do something. Why?"

"Just asking. Getting in your business a lil bit."

He didn't really have anything important to talk about, he just didn't want to miss her too much. Otherwise he wouldn't get much of anything done that day.

"Well, that's probably it babe. I'm never doing anything special. We'll most likely take

MJ to the park and then hit the mall or something."

"You need some money?"

"No. I still have the money you gave me."

"I'm gonna send you some anyway. Do something nice for yourself. Shit, buy something you've always wanted. Something. I feel kind of bad."

Jordyn knew what he felt bad for. She'd been taking care of his kid like she was her own and he hadn't even taken her on a date or anything. He should have felt bad, but she wasn't tripping. Being around him was more than enough for her.

"Okay. If you insist."

"I do." He smiled thinking about how sweet she was. "And one of these days we're gonna go out. Just me and you. I promise to make time for that."

"Whatever you say, Mega."

Jordyn was in LaLa land after they spoke. She was already planning their future dates and what things would be like once they started a family of their own. She was so excited about their future she texted Kaylani about it the entire time she got herself and MJ ready to head out for the day.

They decided to just meet up at the mall and do some shopping. Mega had gone overboard again and sent her another five thousand dollars for whatever reason, so she said what the hell. She might as well shop till she drops.

It was about noon when she made it to the mall. Kaylani liked to get in early, before all the traffic started, just so they could avoid all the niggas that always tried to talk to them. For one, she was gay. And two, she was really trying to see where things were headed between her and Layton. Jordyn felt like she was rushing into something too prematurely, but then again she couldn't talk. She was already head over-heels for a nigga who had a baby with another bitch.

"Bout time you got here. Damn!"

"Girl, my bad. You know I got a baby now and shit."

Kaylani died laughing at that. She was amazed, and so proud, at the way her friend was handling taking care of the next bitch's kid. She gave it to Jordyn, because if that ball was in her court she would've had no idea what to do with it.

"Oh yeah, I forgot about that. Well, what you need me to grab? You want me to hold your baby while you get your lil diaper bag and shit?"

"Yes, please. That would help me out a lot."

MJ seemed pleased to be hanging onto Kaylani. Either that, or she was just a people-person. Jordyn refused to believe that was the case, based on who her parents were.

"Alright now," Kaylani teased as she bounced little MJ on her hip. "Don't have me getting baby fever. Me and your auntie Lay-Lay might have some things to talk about."

"Here you go!" Jordyn laughed. "Your ass dun fell in love over night?"

"I really did. Layton is everything. Oh my god."

After getting MJ locked into her stroller, the diaper bag in check and their cars locked up, the girls headed into the mall. They hadn't even made it out of the parking lot yet and there were already dudes on their heels trying to get their numbers. Jordyn hated that shit. That was why she barely ever went out anywhere. That, and Polo always had her locked in the house.

"What's up with you and Layton? I sent you over there to check on her, not fall in love." Jordyn joked as they took their afternoon stroll through the mall.

"Girl! I had every intention to just check on her, have a little small talk and let it be that, right?"

"Right?"

"But bitch...as soon as she opened that door and I smelled that cologne? I knew I had to make my move. I saw her peeping out the window as I was walking up and I know what freshly sprayed cologne smells like, so I already knew what time it was when I got in there."

Kaylani was getting hot in her panties just thinking about Layton and the chemistry they had. Jordyn could see it written all over her face. She was happy for her friend. Even though she never kept anybody around for too long, Jordyn felt like maybe Layton would be the one to keep her interest.

"I talked to her last night. She sounded like she really likes you." Jordyn chimed in. "She was happy as hell that you were the one I sent over there."

"Was she?" a huge smile crossed Kaylani's face. "She wants me to come over after we finish doing what we doing for the day."

"Good. Go ahead. I'm happy for y'all."

The more Kaylani talked about her and Layton, the more Jordyn thought about what she was doing with Mega. She really really liked him. There was something inside her that woke up every time she heard his name. Pictured his smile. Smelled his cologne. Especially when she looked at MJ.

Kaylani noticed that Jordyn seemed to be spaced out and quickly brought her back to their conversation. She wanted to know what was going on between her and Mega too. Because Jordyn was doing way more wifey shit than she was with Polo, and that was a major concern for her.

"What's going on with this? You. Mega. The baby. The baby mama?"

"Girl." Jordyn sighed and rolled her eyes. "She keeps calling asking him to help her out of the shit she got herself into. She wants him to come to New York, or wherever the fuck she is. I told him to go, but he keeps whining about not wanting to go without me."

"Hold up... he wants you to go with him and you said no? You crazy as hell. If Layton asks me to go with her to meet her ex-bitch I'm definitely going."

"I do sound crazy, right? I don't know, I just want him to be able to figure this shit out with her and not have any distractions. You know? Like you said, they have shit to discuss that doesn't involve me and I can't be there to hold his hand with everything."

"But he wants you there. He doesn't even wanna go if you don't go. That's deep. Shit, maybe I was wrong about him."

And just like that, all of Jordyn's doubts started to fade away. But even that made her more doubtful. She wondered if she was making the right decision by letting herself fall as hard as she had for him. The 'not knowing' really fucked with her head, whether it showed in her actions or not.

While Jordyn was out shopping and Mega was out tattooing, Pauline made her way over to bingo. Not only because her product was in high demand, but also because she loved bingo. She hadn't gone in a few days and started to feel a little lonely again.

When she got there things were quiet. They always were. But, once the games started rolling and more people started pouring in, the noise picked up. She had a strange feeling on her way there. One that didn't go away after she made it either. The entire time she played her cards, and served her clients, she felt like someone was watching her.

She kept looking over her shoulders to make sure no one was actually there and even though she didn't spot anyone suspicious, that feeling just would not go away.

"You okay, Pauline? You look worried?" one of the old women at her table asked.

Pauline almost wondered if she was the one watching her. When she looked up from her cards to take a good look at her, the woman didn't look like she could see much of anything.

"Yeah." Pauline chuckled. "I'm fine. How bout yourself?"

"I'm great. Ready to play my cards and win this money they got waiting on me."

"You gotta get through me first."

Their joking eased Pauline's mind a little. She figured she was just paranoid because of how much money she'd already made and did her best to keep her mind focused on business.

She stayed at the bingo hall for a few more hours, rounding up bingo chips and making her sales. It was nearing six o'clock and the night skies were slowly rolling in. Pauline didn't like being out alone at night, especially with so much cash on her. So, she turned in her cards and made her way towards the street to catch her uber.

As she waited near the curb she got the urge to count her money. Right there on the street. She did it as discreetly as possible, but got a little too excited when she saw that she'd rounded up a little over ten thousand dollars that day.

"Damn old timer," she smiled at herself. "I guess you still got it, huh?"

After shuffling through her bills once more, she stuffed them into her satchel and hid it at the bottom of her purse. Then, there came that feeling again. The feeling of someone watching her. She'd been so caught up in enjoying the smell of money she forgot all about that nagging feeling in her gut. Until it punched her there again and again.

She looked all around her and saw no one. Other than the people walking the streets to get to where they were going. There was a chill in the air while she waited. Something that oddly lingered over her. She kept checking her phone to see how far away her driver was and when the guy finally pulled up to the curb, she nearly broke the handle off of his car trying to hurry up and get inside.

"I take it you're Pauline?"

"That's me. You John?" she asked, double checking the picture on his profile.

"That's me."

"Well, alright then. We're set to go."

As the car pulled away from the curb a dark figure emerged from the shadows of the bingo hall. A small time banger that Pauline had overlooked several times before, because he just didn't look suspicious enough. He'd been tailing her ever since she started slanging down the bingo halls, just waiting for her to slip up. However, it wasn't her money he was after. He wanted her supplier.

Chapter Seventeen

Mega finished up with his client around seven that night. He hadn't been by Layton's since he found out that MJ was his, so he decided he'd drop in and check on her before he hit the highway to head home.

"What up, fool?" Layton answered while she got ready for Kaylani to show up.

"Ain't shit, just leaving the shop. What you doing? I was gonna stop by."

"Ahh, tonight's not a good night. My lil chick on her way over here. You know, I'm trying to get my thug thizzle on."

"Oh shit!" Mega laughed. "You done got yourself into a relationship or some shit?"

"Trying to see where it goes. Shit, I'm trying to get like you! You the one over there playing house."

Hearing those words made shit extra real for Mega because that was exactly what he and Jordyn were doing. Playing house. He didn't necessarily like the way it sounded, but that was what it was. He had just been keeping himself so busy he didn't take the time to actually let the reality set in. Or take the time to spend any real bonding time with his daughter, and something inside him told him that had to change.

"Alright then, I'ma let you get back to falling in love." He laughed. "Hit me up sometime this week so we can get together."

"Alright bet."

As soon as he ended his call with Layton, Jordyn Facetimed him. When he answered he was expecting to see her fine ass on the screen, instead it was MJ. Stirring a pot of pasta.

"Aw man." He smiled at the sight of her. "Jordyn got you over there slaving over a hot stove."

"Yep!" Jordyn chimed in as she made her way onto the screen. "This lil girl gave me a run for my money today. So I'm just returning the favor."

Getting cute messages and picture mail from them was always the highlight of his day. Whether he mentioned it or not. Sometimes, when he was feeling doubtful, he would scroll through his gallery looking at pictures of them as a pick-me-up.

"She look like she know what she doing too. What y'all making?"

"Shrimp scampi. You know that's my favorite. I was gonna stop and grab some takeout, but it was still a little early when we got back, so I decided to cook instead."

"You cooking for me too? I'm hungry."

"I'm surprised you ain't already ate. You be acting like you don't wanna have dinner with me sometimes. What, I be smacking too much?"

"Nah!" He laughed. "I just be tired by the time I get home. Save me some though. I'ma stop at the lil bar on the way and have a drink. Then I'll be there."

"Okay. Don't be out all night."

Pauline smelled the Scampi cooking as soon as she walked in from bingo and already knew what Jordyn was up to.

"I can smell the scampi from the driveway." She chuckled, stopping into the kitchen before heading to her room. "I should've never let you order off the adult menu as a lil girl."

"Yep! You shouldn't have." Jordyn laughed. "Mama! The first time you took me to Paris and that lady came over there with those big old shrimp, I knew that was gon be my favorite thing to eat for the rest of my life."

"And you weren't lying."

Pauline thought back to all the traveling they did back in the day. She wanted to get back into that. The money she planned to start bringing in again would allow it, so she didn't see why they shouldn't.

"We should do that again before I get too old."

Jordyn knew what her mother was getting at. She was scared they wouldn't have time to do many things before her cancer really crippled her for good.

"I'm down for that." Jordyn smiled. "It's been a while since we've gone anywhere."

"It has. I'm sorry that things are so different now. I should've done better as a mother."

"Ma," Jordyn waved her off. "Don't talk like that. You did what you had to do. We all make mistakes. As long as we learn from them and do better, moving forward is all that matters."

It was a wonder to Pauline how her daughter turned out so strong and insightful. She thought for sure Jordyn would grow up spoiled and bitter, but that wasn't her. She was sweet as pie and would do whatever she could to keep positive energy flowing. Truth be told, Pauline learned a lot through being Jordyn's mom.

"You right, baby. You are absolutely right."

The older woman walked over to hug and kiss her daughter. And also greet MJ, who was blowing spit bubbles and wiggling her fingers at her.

"She wants you." Jordyn leaned in to hand her MJ.

"Oo, I gotta set my purse down for this. You a big ol' youngin."

Once Pauline sat her purse down on the table, she shuffled back over to hold MJ. She was a big baby, and Jordyn saw exactly why. Her daddy was stalky as hell and loved to eat.

"Oh my god, thank you." Jordyn took a breath of relief. "That girl would not let me put her down all day today. Heavy self."

"Aww. She just wanted to be held."

"I guess so. She usually wants to scoot around and do her own thing, but today she wanted to be right up under me for some reason."

"You think she starting to look at you as mama?"

That question almost made Jordyn choke on her own breath. She hoped that wasn't the case. Not because she didn't care for MJ in that way, but she really wasn't trying to take over Mila's role in her daughter's life.

"Ma, don't say that. Of course not." She replied unsurely.

"I'm just saying." Pauline shrugged. "You are the one there taking care of her from sun up to sun down. And once kids start to grow that comfort for someone they do get deeply attached."

Facetiming with Jordyn and MJ had Mega eager to get back home. Being alone in the car with his music blasting had his mind wondering. He started thinking about his bond with MJ. It wasn't as strong as it should have been and if he was always ripping and running the way he was, it never would be.

He didn't want the type of relationship with his own kid that he had with his father growing up. Nonexistent. MJ didn't deserve that. She deserved to be cared for and loved. Spoiled and nurtured. The same things he wanted as a child. He was mad at Mila for making him miss out on so much time with her, but also mad at himself that he was still letting that time pass him by.

Instead of going to the bar like he planned to, he decided to stop at a liquor store and stock up on some bottles. As he walked through the store pushing a cart full of clinking bottles, he noticed the same guy on every aisle. At first, he thought nothing of it because trouble rarely followed him. Then, he thought maybe the guy was some undercover loss prevention worker making sure he didn't steal anything. But after getting the strangest feeling of knowing the guy, Mega's senses were on high alert.

"Someone throwing a party?" the cashier asked as he scanned Mega's massive haul of alcohol.

"I guess you could say that." Mega said, pretending to check his phone.

When he saw the guy who had followed him through the store standing behind him in line, he knew for sure the guy wasn't loss prevention. He thought about turning around and asking the guy what his problem was, but figured he'd wait to see if he made a move once they were outside.

"Is that everything for you?" the cashier asked, before reading him his total.

"Yeah, that's it."

After paying his tab and loading all of his bags into his cart, Mega headed for the exit. He calmly strolled over to his Jeep and started loading his bags up, keeping his eyes focused on his surroundings the entire time. It wasn't long before the guy behind him came out the door and headed towards a dark colored SUV parked across the parking lot.

"Niggas acting mad weird out here tonight." Mega mumbled to himself. "I hope this motherfucker ready to die if he play crazy."

Just to buy some time and see where their encounter was headed, Mega walked his cart back to the front of the store. He figured, if the guy wasn't a creep and only there to buy liquor, he would get in his car and drive away. Lo-and-behold, the guy was still sitting in the parking lot when Mega got back to his Jeep.

For a moment they locked eyes and just sat there, staring at each other from across the parking lot. It became more than evident what the guy was there for, Mega just didn't know why. Or who he was. Unphased, he turned on his ignition and waited a moment longer. The guy did the same.

"Alright, motherfucker." Mega spoke as if the guy could hear him. "You wanna play? Let's play."

Easing his Jeep onto the road outside the parking lot, Mega cranked up his music and cruised without a care in the world. When he saw the black SUV hit the street behind him from his rearview mirror, he hit the gas and raced onto the highway. The black SUV did the same.

They both revved their engines in and out of traffic, racing from side of the highway to the next. It had been a while since Mega floored an engine as hard as he was that night, but he still had it. He got his experience driving when he ran drugs as a teenager. His drops always had to be to the dock by a certain time and the only way he knew how to get them there before the deadline was speeding. Something he loved to do.

"Let's go!" He shouted as he let off the gas a little for his opp to catch up. "What you got for me nigga!?" He laughed.

The driver of the black SUV was no match for the man he was chasing. It made Mega wonder who the fuck even sent him. It had to be someone who only wanted to send a message, because anybody who wanted any real results would've had him dead before he left the parking lot.

Their game of cat and mouse lasted about two exits longer. And to put a little distance between them, Mega shot off the exit and sped towards an old secluded truck stop not too far off. He raced into the parking lot and quickly got out of his Jeep before he saw the headlights of the SUV pull in a minute later.

His Jeep wasn't hard to spot. Everybody in South Florida knew who he was when they saw it coming, so he knew the guy would know where to find him. Thing was, Mega was already two steps ahead of him. He had a gun aimed at his temple before he even had time to put his shit in park.

"Put the window down." Mega said, ready to lick a shot to the niggas dome.

The window came down on command. When he saw the dudes face up close and personal, he already knew who had sent him.

"Give me the keys."

The driver looked at him like he was crazy.

"My keys?"

"You heard me, nigga. Give me the motherfucking keys before I open your shit up right here in this parking lot."

The slight grin on Mega's face let the guy know he wasn't bullshitting, and he did what the hell he was told. All of Bossy's men were afraid of him, but none of them were ready to die behind him.

"Tell Bossy I'm not interested."

Chapter Eighteen

Mega took his time getting home after his race war. He wanted to be sure he didn't bring home any unwanted guests because he didn't realize anyone else was following him. After figuring out the dude from the parking lot belonged to Bossy, he knew some shit was bound to go down. He had a strange feeling in his gut about it.

It was way after midnight before he pulled into the driveway. He didn't bother texting Jordyn back because by the time he checked his phone, he was already home. He knew she had an attitude, but Mega was more concerned about their safety before anything.

Instead of sitting down to eat he went straight upstairs to tell her what happened. When he got there, she and MJ were already passed out in bed. Jordyn was lying on her side and MJ was sprawled out right next to her. He smiled when he looked down at the drooling baby sleeping comfortably in his bed, and couldn't believe that she belonged to him.

"Come here." He whispered as he lifted her from her sleepy slumber.

He couldn't help but hold her tight and snuggle up against her. It felt like holding a newborn bundle of love. Mega lightly rocked his daughter in his arms as he slowly walked around the room, taking in her baby lavender scent. His heart felt so light and fluffy while he held her, he would've held her close all night if Jordyn hadn't woken up.

She sat up in bed when she didn't feel MJ lying next to her and almost panicked. Until she saw Mega cradling her in his arms. The visual completely melted her heart and all the anger and doubt she felt for him that night was quickly washed away.

"Take her to her bed," she whispered into the dimness of the room. "She needs to get used to staying in it at night."

He wasn't ready to end his bonding session with his kid, but Jordyn had her on a schedule and he didn't want to take her away from that. It amazed him how serious she was when it came to parenting MJ. He almost wondered if she didn't have some secret kids of her own hiding out somewhere.

"I'm sorry I was out so long." He said, when he came back from putting MJ down. "I ran into some trouble on my way."

Jordyn's eyebrows nearly crawled off her face when she heard the word trouble. The last time trouble came their way they almost died.

"What happened?"

"Instead of going to the bar I stopped at the liquor store so I could just come straight home. When I got there I noticed some nigga following me. I sat in the parking lot for a minute, just to be sure I wasn't being paranoid, but nah. The nigga was following me."

"Who was he?"

"Remember that gay Puerto Rican dude? The one who's been trying to get me to do business with him?"

"The one my dad works for?"

"Yeah. One of his dudes."

Jordyn got the chills when she thought about them finding out where Mega lived. If Bossy was anything like her father, he would find out sooner or later. Especially if he was that adamant about getting Mega to push his weight.

"So, what? He thinks he can just bully you into working for him?"

"I don't know what he thinking, but I ain't going. I work for me and me alone."

"You think he might know where to find you now?"

"I mean, if I'm at the shop maybe. Everybody knows where my shop is. I'm guessing that's where the dude followed me from cause I didn't go anywhere else. And I made sure I drove around for a while once I lost him, to make sure nobody else was following me home."

The way Mega's mind worked turned Jordyn on. The way he talked about his life and how he handled business. She loved hearing about it at times, but sometimes it scared her too. His life was literally like a movie, and she'd seen so many crime movies it wasn't hard for her to picture how it all could end.

"You scare me, Mega." She said, wrapping her arms around him from behind. "I be so worried about you not making it home to this kid."

He sat in silence as he rested his chin down on her arm. She had a point. Things could have easily turned out completely different for him that night if Bossy really wanted it to. He had to be more aware. More careful. Especially for his kid.

"Me too."

"You need to be careful." She spoke lightly. "Keep your eyes open at all times. Make sure you let someone know where you're going.

Even if it's just me or Layton. Mecca needs her father in her life. Her mother too."

It pained her to think about Mila, but her womanhood wouldn't let her be unfair to her. Mila was MJ's mother and she deserved to be in her life just as much as anyone else. Her leaving was for the good of her daughter's safety, and Jordyn couldn't let that go unnoticed.

"Are you coming with me to see her?" he asked, turning around to see her face.

She sighed and sat back against the pillows on the bed and just like she knew he would, Mega crawled right into her arms.

"Do you think that's a good idea?" she asked, as she caressed his head. "I don't wanna be a distraction for you while y'all figure out whatever it is you need to."

His guilty conscience made it sound like Jordyn had been reading his mind about the way he felt for Mila. He still wasn't even sure what that was. She was only talking about how they would get her out of the shit she was in and how they were going to parent MJ, it just felt like she knew he thought about more than that.

"I want you to come. You been helping me cope with this whole situation a lot, I don't know. I feel like I need you there. I'm not worried about how she'll feel about it. If that's what you're worried about."

"No, I just wanna be fair to her. I'm not trying to step on her toes or nothing like that."

"I get you. But shit, she actually owes you a huge thank you. I mean, yeah I know she gon be mad and shit, but that's her problem."

The way he talked about the situation put Jordyn's mind at ease a little. He didn't sound like he was unsure of where he and Mila stood, but that was something Jordyn secretly worried about at times.

"Maybe me and her will sit down and talk one day. I owe her an apology too."

"You a real stand up woman, you know that?" he asked, sitting up in front of her.

Jordyn got bashful when he looked deep into her eyes. The amount of attention he paid to her was unreal. She'd never had a man uplift her the way Mega did.

"I try to be. I mean, I just know how I want to be treated, so." She shrugged.

He leaned in and kissed her. She really made everything feel like it was going to be alright for him. Even the shit with Bossy. He didn't know how, or why he felt that way, when Jordyn wasn't even in the game. Her nurturing nature just brought him a lot of comfort.

"What was that for?"

"I don't know. Maybe I like you or something."

"Oh yeah?" she asked, smiling at his playfulness. "I hope so, because I like you too."

"Good." He kissed her again. "I'm gonna go take a shower."

When Mega went into the bathroom, Jordyn decided to go downstairs and pour herself a glass of wine. She heard Pauline shuffling around in her room and went down the hall to poke her head in. The door was cracked and when she saw a huge pile of cash spread out all over the bed, she walked right in.

"Ma, what the hell?"

"What?" Pauline nonchalantly sat down in her chair.

"What are you doing with all of this?"

"I made it at bingo."

"Bingo? Yeah, I bet."

Pauline wasn't exactly lying. She did make her money at bingo, in more ways than one.

"I did." She chuckled. "What you doing up?"

"Just came down for a glass of wine. Mega woke me up coming in all late."

"Everything okay?"

Jordyn sighed. She was sitting in the middle of her mothers bed with her legs crossed, like she used to as a kid whenever they talked. Everything felt okay, but she was still feeling a little unsure. No matter how much Mega told her not to worry about Mila, she couldn't help but to worry.

"I don't know, ma. I hope they are."

"What you worried about, baby girl?"

"Everything. Mila. Mega. life. You. I just don't wanna be tied down to another man who ain't gon do nothing but break my heart. "

Pauline was a little triggered by that. The thought of her daughter being hurt by any man was one she couldn't bear. She knew exactly what that felt like because she'd been there one too many times.

"Do you feel like he might be lying to you about his feelings for her? Or you?"

"It's hard to tell. When he talks about her he sounds like he doesn't care about her at all. That's where I'm confused. I mean, I know they have a kid together and everything, but is that the only reason he wants to help her? This is the same chick Polo cheated on me with and I don't wanna go down that road again."

"Baby," Pauline sighed. "Dealing with men can be very tricky. Some words of advice that I've always tried to live by: How you get the man, is usually how you'll lose him. I hate to think that way about Mega, because he is a good man, but men also have feelings. Feelings that a lot of them don't know how to express until it's too late."

Jordyn was familiar with the saying: how you got them was usually how you lost them. She just didn't want that to be the case for her and Mega. She even asked herself if she would be able to stick around if he decided he wanted to work things out with Mila for the sake of their baby.

Sadly, she felt like she would take him back if things didn't work out between them and she didn't want that for herself. She knew she deserved better than that.

"Thanks for the talk, ma." She said, getting up to hug her mother goodnight.

"Any time, baby. And you remember what I always taught you? Don't be like me, be what?"

"Be better."

Before heading back upstairs, Jordyn sat at the table in silence and finished her wine. Her feelings were hurting and she didn't even know why. Nothing had happened, yet there was something in her gut that didn't feel right. She wanted to talk to Mega about it, but didn't want him to feel like she didn't trust him or was accusing him of anything.

She figured she would just wait it out and see. If Mila was who he wanted to be with there was nothing she could do about it. History always weighed the most when it came to relationships. No matter how toxic the situation was. The heart wants what the heart wants, no matter what.

"You okay?"

"Yeah. Just went down for a glass of wine and to clear my head." She said, as she climbed back into bed. "Go to sleep."

Chapter Nineteen

It was around noon when Mega rolled out of bed the next day. Jordyn was downstairs hanging out at the pool with MJ and Pauline was already gone to bingo. The house was quiet, leaving Mega with nothing but his thoughts to fill the silence.

He thought about Jordyn and her mood change before going to bed. Something was bothering her and he felt like he already knew what it was. It bothered him too, but he was mad at himself for letting the shit trickle down to Jordyn. He hated the thought of her being hurt behind his foolishness with Mila. It wasn't fair to her.

After taking a few puffs of his blunt, he went downstairs to join them at the pool. MJ was in her lifejacket having the time of her life, while Jordyn sipped on her Mai Tai and snapped pictures on her phone. He wondered if she was posting them on Instagram or Facebook, and how many niggas she probably had in her inbox. When he realized that he was being a little bit jealous, he laughed at himself and stepped outside to join her in the pool.

"Look who's awake." She smiled at MJ. "And he's finally coming to hang out with us."

MJ squealed and splashed the water around her when she saw him getting into the pool. She was such a happy baby, it made Mega feel proud to have a kid who enjoyed life. That proudness made him want to be present more and more.

"Is this what y'all do when I'm gone? Cause I can get down with this." He said, as he swam out to MJ.

"Sometimes. Sometimes we watch movies and play games. Sometimes we order a bunch of junk food and snack until we fall asleep. I try to keep her little self busy a lot, otherwise she gets cranky. I guess she's just like you. Always on the go."

"I'm trying to do better. I wanna be around more. I missed a whole year of her life already, I don't wanna be that dad who just provides and doesn't really spend time with his kids."

"Kids? How many of these do you have?" Jordyn joked.

"How many you wanna have?"

His question gave her butterflies. She'd never been asked that question before. Not by a man she was dating at least.

"You think you wanna have kids with me?" she asked, just to see where his emotions were.

"Maybe." He shrugged. "I mean, ain't that what people do when they find somebody they wanna settle down with?"

"It is." She smiled and sipped her drink.

Watching him play in the pool with MJ made Jordyn fall more in love than she already was. There was nothing like a man who loved his kids and had plans for the future. A future that included her. She wanted to cry, she was so happy.

The three of them splashed around the pool for a couple more hours, until MJ got sleepy and was ready for her nap. Jordyn left Mega in charge of getting her fed, washed up and in her crib. While Jordyn showered and had herself some much needed me-time. It wasn't that hard of a task for him. He'd helped his mom raise his siblings growing up, so he knew what to do as far as putting a baby to sleep.

"Out like a light." He sang, proud of himself for getting her to sleep so smoothly.

"Good job." Jordyn laughed and clapped her hands. "Not as bad as you thought it would be, huh?"

"Nah, it's not. She's a cool kid."

"Yeah she is."

He dreaded having to tell her he had another meeting to go to. Their day had started off so perfect all he wanted to do was cuddle up with her, eat, and watch movies all day. However, duty called and he had obligations to tend to.

"I gotta step out for a lil bit."

Disappointment washed over Jordyn's face. He hated it because he knew what it felt like. All the times his dad told him he was coming and never showed up came flashing back into his mind. It made him feel like he was doing the same thing to Jordyn.

"I won't be gone long. I promise. I'm just going to meet with another new connect then I'm coming right back home."

"Okay." She said, nonchalantly.

He hated the way her answer came out. She sounded so dry, it was like she almost didn't care whether he came home or not. He didn't want her to stop caring about him and grow distant, but he understood that a woman had needs of her own too.

"You wanna come with me?"

"What?" she scrunched up her face. "No I don't wanna come with you. That's not my thing. And I have MJ."

"She can come too."

"No! What the fuck, Mega. She is not going around no shit like that. Are you crazy?"

He laughed at how overprotective she was of MJ already. It was only a joke, he just wanted to get a reaction out of her to lighten the mood.

"I'm just playing." He said, hugging her from behind.

"Don't play like that. You bout to get snapped on."

"Snap on me later." He kissed her neck and pressed up against her butt. "Like, for real, for real. Snap."

When she caught on to what he was saying she laughed and bumped him away with her butt.

"You're so nasty. Manish. Dirty. Slutty!" She laughed as he headed out the door.

"And you love it, so I don't even know why you tripping." He smiled. "I'll see you in a few."

"Mhm."

It was so easy for him to make her forget about being mad. He didn't even have to try hard either. There was just something so genuine about him that put all of her worries to rest. She wondered how long it would last, though. Having a nice life and loads of money wasn't what attracted her to him, so it sure in hell wasn't going to keep her.

It was about Six o'clock when Mega got to the restaurant he was scheduled to meet with his new connect. He didn't see the guy he was supposed to be meeting with yet, so he sat at the bar and ordered a drink. He also let his eyes roam around the building to see if he would spot any familiar faces.

Everyone in attendance was dressed down in suit and tie, Mega included, and the vibes were nice and classy. He thought about taking Jordyn back for dinner one night. Those were the kinds of places he liked to go whenever he needed to wind down. Unlike a lot of guys his age, Mega had a vision for himself. He wasn't stuck up or anything, but he did love the finer things in life. The Bacharachs and Par-ee's of the world.

After about fifteen more minutes of waiting for his people to show up, they finally did. The guy was an older guy. Looked like he was straight off the boat from Cuba. He had two younger men with him, whom Mega figured were his bodyguards or some shit. Nothing unordinary jumped out at him, so he made his way over to their table.

"Mr. Navarro." The older gentleman spoke, in a heavy Cuban accent. "A pleasure to finally meet you. And look at him boys!" he gestured towards the two men he had in tow. "He knows how to wear a suit. Please, have a seat."

The first thought that popped into Mega's mind was "Don't tell me he's gay." He'd had enough of men hitting on him thanks to Bossy.

"Mr. Quintana. Nice to meet you as well."

"Well spoken too." Quintana nodded and removed his hat. "I can see why you are the king of Miami."

"Oh," Mega laughed a little. "I wouldn't call myself the king. I just know how to do business."

"I respect a modest man."

The two guys that came with Mr. Quintana didn't talk much. They seemed to be checking Mega out, which wasn't unusual at all for him. He did the same thing whenever he came across a new business partner.

"How about we order some dinner. Some wine. I'll send these guys away and then we can talk business. Is that okay for you?"

"That's fine with me."

Although Mega was sure the old man had done some unspeakable things in his days as a king-pin, he got good vibes from him. He was actually enjoying sitting across the table from someone twice his senior sharing insight. He didn't know many young drug dealers who were capable of that.

Mr. Quintana liked him too. Mega reminded him of the son he once had. He also liked the fact that Mega was book smart. Being only street smart didn't take many men as far as they wanted to go in their profession.

Mega had only gone to the meeting with the thought of gaining a new supplier in mind. However, Mr. Quintana was looking for someone to pass down his empire to. He would supply Mega with all the dope he could handle, and at a competitive price if that was all he wanted, but the old man wanted more than that himself. Mega was the one he wanted to run his business once he became too ill to keep it afloat.

"Do you know why I wanted to meet with you, young man?" Quintana asked, as he shoveled the last of his bloody steak into his old wrinkly mouth.

"I figured we were going to discuss competitive pricing." Mega replied, getting a little anxious. "Is there something else you wanted from me?"

Mr. Quintana carefully dabbed his mouth with his napkin and leaned back in his chair.

"Is that all you wanted to discuss?" the old man asked.

"I'm not sure what you're getting at." Mega dabbed his mouth with his napkin and did the same.

"I'll be blunt with you. I want you to take over my business. How you run it will be strictly up to you, but you're the only one I trust."

Mega laughed, thinking the old man was just fucking with him, but he was serious.

"Crazy right?" Quintana lifted his wine glass from the table. "You and I have never crossed paths. Done a lot of business, unbeknownst to us both, but we've never formally met, and you're the only one I trust."

"That does sound crazy." Mega agreed, leaning into the table for a little privacy. "Are you demented or something?"

"Demented!" Mr. Quintana burst into laughter. His goons heard him from across the room and got ready to rush over, but the old man swiftly waved a hand and sat them back down. "Demented? No. I do have other health issues that raise my eyebrows though. Which is why I'm looking for someone to take over. I wanna spend whatever time I have left with my family. I also want them to be able to maintain their lifestyle should anything happen to me. All in all, I'm just getting too old to be in the game anymore."

Mega wondered if it was some kind of set up. He'd heard of guys quickly trying to pass off their empires once they got in trouble with the law. There were also guys who set up deals with the jakes to save their ass if they were facing time. But, he had also heard a lot about Mr. Quintana in his days. Word had it the man was a real OG and as solid as they came, so him working with the law wasn't something Mega thought about too hard.

"You knew my son. JR."

The wheels in Mega's head started to turn. He remembered a JR. his face didn't pop into his head right away, until he took a real long look at the man sitting across from him.

"No shit." A huge smile slid across his face. "JR Quintana was your son? I called him Q."

"That's right." The old man got teary eyed. "He made me call him that shit too." He laughed. "I hated it."

Memories flooded both of their minds. Mega thought back to the last time he saw JR. Had he known that would've been the last time they saw each other he would've taken him up on that titty bar offer.

"I'm sorry about what happened to him. Your son and I were really close. He was the only man I trusted for a long time."

"Yeah," Mr. Quintana nodded. "He told me all about you. He also told me that if I ever needed help to come to you. That you are the only man I should trust."

Hearing such a great review from a man so well respected made Mega feel like maybe he was the king of Miami.

"Wow." He nodded, grabbing his glass to toast to his long lost friend. "That really means a lot to me. I didn't know he felt that way."

"My son respected you a lot. He said you were like the brother he never had. It pains me to know that we didn't get to spend as much time as we should have before he was killed, but I try to celebrate his life everyday."

Mega leaned in and shook the man's hand to pay homage. If he could go back in time and make that drop with JR, he was sure things would have gone a different way. JR had been trying to get Mega to join him and his dad's work for years, but he was too headstrong. Mega wanted to build his own empire.

"Can I ask you a personal question?" Quintana said, pouring himself another glass of wine.

"Yes, sir."

"What are your dealings with Bossy?"

"Bossy?" Mega asked, confused. "We don't have any dealings. One of his men came after me not too long ago and he was supposed to take care of that."

"Charles?"

Mr. Quintana could read the suspicion in Mega's eyes. He wanted to know how he knew as much as he knew.

"I'm gonna give you a heads up. Bossy' wants you to push his product for him. He's falling off, bad. His own family won't even touch him. Ever since his father passed away and left him in charge he's been on some type of power trip. A lot of people have backed away from him so he's not being able to pay the bills on time. I wouldn't trust him if I were you."

"I don't trust him at all. That's why I declined his business proposition."

"Well he's adamant about getting to you. He's been asking around about you a lot."

Rage filled Mega's blood. He always kept a low profile, so Bossy asking around about him was bad for business. He didn't want his name to ring any more bells than it already had.

Chapter Twenty

Before bingo the next day, Pauline stopped at her favorite caribbean food spot to grab some grub. She had a few customers to meet up with there as well. After placing her order, she took a seat at the back of the restaurant to wait. The owner knew her fairly well, so they didn't mind her little transactions being done on the inside. So long as she broke them off a piece of her profit at the end of each week.

"Paulie D." The owner came hobbling from behind the counter with her food in hand. "It's payday, my lady." He said, in his heavy Jamaican accent.

"I know what day it is, Gene. I got your envelope right here, baby." She teased him with a fluffy brown envelope.

"How you doing today?"

"I'm alright. Hanging in there. How bout yourself?"

The owner had some concerns about her. He'd gotten word from one of his employees that Pauline had a stalker and wanted to be sure that her eyes and ears were open.

"I'm doing just fine." He said, sticking the envelope into his inside pocket. "I'm a little concerned about you, though. You ain't had no run ins or anything have you?"

Pauline quickly thought back to that strange feeling she had in her gut at bingo.

"No. But, I've been having the strangest feeling lately. Like - I don't know, like someone's been watching me."

"Listen to your gut, my lady. One of my employees told me the other day he saw a guy looking at you kind of funny. Like he'd been watching you for some time now."

"I knew it! All day at bingo I felt like someone was watching me. Following me even. Did he say who he was?"

No one suspected popped into mind right away. She didn't have any enemies in Miami, she barely even knew anyone. The majority of her customers were older people, so she was sure she would've been able to spot one of them if they were following her. Then again, she couldn't be sure.

"He said the guy didn't look familiar. You know we get a lot of traffic in and around this place, so any of us would know him if he was a regular. Maybe someone from out of town?"

"Maybe."

A worried look came across Pauline's face. She thought about all the money she'd fucked up back in the day and wondered if someone from her past had sent someone to get her. Then she thought about Charles. She knew it wasn't him because he wasn't described as "some big nigga". Truth be told, Pauline had no idea who the person could've been. She figured it had to be someone she'd sold to recently, because who else would it be?

"Well Gene, thanks for the heads up. I gotta get out of here and get to bingo. They waiting on me down there."

"Alright. You be careful."

"I will."

Leaving the restaurant, Pauline had an eerie feeling. She texted Jordyn, and Mega, just to let them know what she'd been told. In case anything happened to her. Jordyn wanted her to come home immediately, while Mega left the shop to head over to the bingo hall where she said she was going.

"Mega, please make her come home. Either that, or I'm going up there to get her."

"Calm down. I'm on my way over there now. I'll take care of it."

Jordyn was a nervous wreck. She was so nervous she was already in the car ready to pull out of the garage. Mega didn't want her to leave the house and risk anyone following her, so he made her stay where she was.

When Pauline got to the bingo hall she hurried up and dashed inside. Mega's shop wasn't far from where Pauline played bingo, so he was already sitting in the parking lot waiting for her to arrive. When she got there and ran inside, he immediately spotted the man who had been following her. It was the same black SUV that had followed him nights before. The same driver too.

The driver of the SUV didn't spot Mega, because he wasn't driving his Jeep that day. He was sitting in the parking lot of the bingo hall, seemingly waiting for Pauline to come back out.

"Did she make it there?" Jordyn called him to inquire.

"Yeah, she's inside. I'm sitting in the parking lot now. I know the guy who's following her. It's the same nigga that followed me the oher night."

"What the fuck? Well, what does he want with my mom?"

"Probably trying to use her to get to me."

"You gotta get her out of there before something happens to her. I can't take it if something happens to her."

"Jordyn, I'm not gon let nothing happen to your mom. Trust me. I got her. I'll call you when we leave. Start packing for New York."

Jordyn wanted them to leave right then, but Mega had other plans. He wanted to wait it out and see what the guy would do. If he would bring Bossy out of the backseat or some shit. If he did, Mega was planning to kill him dead right there in the parking lot.

About an hour passed before Mega saw Pauline's favorite Uber driver pull into the front of the building. She must've gotten spooked and called him to swing by early. Before she made it outside the driver of the SUV approached the guys car. Mega saw him hand him a few bills and tell him to get out of there, that's when Mega made his move.

He crept into the back of the bingo hall and made his way towards the playroom. When he spotted Pauline, he calmly walked over to her table and took a seat.

"What you doing here, young blood?" she asked, happy to see a trustworthy face.

"Your company is outside."

"What? The guy that's been following me."

"Yeah. I ran into the same guy a few nights ago. He's one of your ex-husband's co-workers."

A chill ran through Pauline's body. She hated the thought of Charles knowing where to find her.

"Where is he?"

"Outside waiting for you to come out. I watched him pay your Uber driver to leave."

"Shit."

"Don't worry about it. I'll take care of him. And Bossy."

Mega wanted Bossy gone off the map. He was making a lot of moves that overstepped a lot of boundaries and that wasn't how the streets worked. Mega minded his business and expected everybody else to do the same. He wasn't exactly sure where Bossy was from, or how they did business there, but stepping on toes wasn't going to work in Mega's territory. All bets were off.

"Let's get out of here."

"You don't have to tell me twice."

Instead of going out the back, they went out the front. Mega wanted the guy to know how sloppy of a job he did tailing her. He also wanted him to relay another message to Bossy.

He let Pauline exit the building first and when she did, the man stepped from the shadows of the bingo hall and grabbed her. As soon as his hand touched her collar, Mega clocked him with the butt of his glock. When the man hit the floor, he quickly bent down and cut off two of his fingers.

The entire bingo hall heard the screams of agony and started rushing towards the front of the building. That was when Mega grabbed Pauline and headed for the parking lot. Once they were in his car he quickly backed out and sped onto the street before anyone saw which car they were in.

"You cut off his fingers." She said, frozen with fear.

"Yeah." He said, tossing the fingers out the window. "The next time I see him he's dead. Now he knows I ain't bullshitting."

Pauline was scared to death. It wasn't like she had never been around violence, or been violent herself, it was the way Mega did it. He was quick, smooth, and nonchalant about it. That let her know that if the situation called for it, he could be a stone-cold-killer.

Their ride home was silent until he pulled into the drive-way. They sat in the car for a moment, not saying a word to each other, before he finally opened his mouth to let her know the plans for the rest of their week. He and Jordyn were headed to New York and she was going to be staying in his mom's guesthouse.

"How long will y'all be gone?"

"I don't know." He sighed. "I gotta handle this shit with Bossy before." He paused, not wanting to say the words.

"I already know." Pauline patted his shoulder, letting him know he didn't have to say it. "End it. However long it takes. Whatever it takes."

Chapter Twenty-One

Jordyn had their bags waiting by the door when they got inside. Mega had already booked their flights to New York, all they had to do was get Pauline packed up and ready to go.

"Ma!" She ran into her mothers arms like a terrified little girl. "You okay?"

"I'm fine. A little shaken up, but I'm okay. You okay?"

"Yeah." Jordyn let out a sigh of relief. "I was scared as hell though."

While Jordyn went to help her mom pack, Mega set his focus on MJ. he took her upstairs to get her dressed and grab the extra's he needed to take with them. He also made a call to Big Shaun to let him know they were on the way.

"What up, homie?" The big man answered on the first ring.

"I'm on a flight out there tonight. You got eyes on Mila yet?"

"Nah, I ain't seen her. I went to the spot you told me she was gonna be, but she wasn't there. Must've got spooked."

"Probably. I'll hit her up and see what's what. I'll let you know what time my flight lands once I get to the airport so you can meet us there."

"Alright, homie. See you then."

Mega got a strange feeling after Big Shaun told him Mila was MIA. They hadn't spoken to each other since she told him where she was. He wondered why the sudden change of plans. If she wasn't in New York anymore he needed to know that before he went all the way out there. And if she had other plans he needed to know that too. In case he had to kill her.

"Yeah?" She answered her phone on the first ring.

"Where are you? My guy said you weren't where you said you were and I ain't heard from you."

"Yeah…. I thought you might've been setting me up, so I left."

"Setting you up?" he laughed, sarcastically. "I think that's more your speed."

"Look Mega, I don't know what the fuck to think these days. I can't trust nobody, so excuse me if I'm looking out for myself."

"Whatever. Anyway, I'm on my way out there. My plane lands tonight. I'm bringing Jordyn and the baby with me cause some shit went down out here and I ain't leaving them behind. So, you need to make sure you're at the airport before our flight touches down. And no bullshit, Mila. I'm not in the mood."

"Why is she coming?" Mila frowned. "She ain't got nothing to do with nothing."

"Yeah she does. And I'm not leaving her. I'll let you know what time the flight is landing. Be there."

Mega hung up the phone before Mila could reply. He really wasn't in the mood to listen to her complain and talk shit about Jordyn coming to New York. Besides, if they were going to be planning their get-back, they would need a babysitter. Somebody they could trust. He wasn't leaving MJ with her mom. Especially not after someone had been following him.

On his way back to MJ's room he heard Jordyn and Pauline talking. He couldn't really make out everything they were saying, but something felt off to him. He was worried about Pauline. There hadn't been much business talk between them since they left Immokalaee. She hadn't been talking about the moves she'd been making at bingo either.

He wondered how the driver of the SUV knew where to find her. They were never out in public together. No one knew where he lived, or that she was staying with him. So it made him question where else Pauline had been hanging out at. Or who else she might have been serving. If she was being caught on to as easily as she had been, she wasn't someone he could have on his team.

"What time are we heading to the airport?" Jordyn asked.

"The flight boards at 7. We should be heading out now to drop your mom off."

"Okay. I think I have everything we need packed and ready to go. I need more milk for MJ."

A slight smile crossed his face when she talked about what she needed for MJ. However, there was something Mega wanted to know about her mom. He just didn't know how to ask her about it.

"What's wrong? You okay?" She asked, sensing a heaviness in his mood.

"I'm good. Just got something on my mind."

"Well, what is it?" She took a seat next to him on the bed.

"Your mom."

The look he gave her when he said that made Jordyn's heart race. She didn't know what she expected him to tell her about her mother, but whatever it was sounded serious.

"Okay? What about her?"

"Has she…." he paused to make sure he said what he wanted to say without too much force. "Has she ever….has she ever been on drugs? Or is she using now? Anything other than weed?"

Jordyn didn't know how to feel about him asking her that. Her mother had been clean for over twenty years and it took a lot for her to get that far. So, Mega's question felt like a slap in the face to Jordyn.

"Why would you ask me that?"

"I'm not tryna offend you or anything. I just….I don't know. I'm tryna piece together how that guy knew where to find her and I can't figure it out."

"Are you implying that she's hanging out with addicts? Or she's working for Bossy?" Jordyn let out a laugh that told Mega she was offended. "I mean, what is it? Do you want us to leave or something? You don't have to accuse my mother of being on drugs to say that. She's been clean for over twenty years. Don't discredit her recovery like that. And she's definitely not the type of person who would try to set anybody up. She has enough problems of her own already."

After giving Mega a piece of her mind she tried to storm out of the room, but he quickly caught up to her and pulled her back inside to apologize. He really wasn't trying to offend her, or discredit Pauline's recovery, but things didn't add up. And if she was in some kind of trouble, or hanging out in places she shouldn't have, that would be an issue for all of them. Something he was trying his best to avoid.

"Ay, I'm sorry." He said, holding onto her from behind. "I'm just tryna make sure we good. I'm only one man and I can't have my eyes everywhere at once. I'm just being safe."

Jordyn calmed down, realizing that she may have overreacted. He was only one man. The only man who had ever had her, and her mothers, well-being in mind. Mega was under a lot of pressure. She had to calm herself down enough to understand that.

"I'm sorry too." She said, turning around to hug him. "I'm sorry. I just get so defensive whenever her recovery is brought up. She struggled with drugs for a long time. I watched her bounce back from hell and get her life right, so I know drugs will be the last thing I'll ever have to worry about. I don't even like her smoking weed."

"I understand." Mega nodded. "Come on, we gotta go."

He loaded their bags into his car while Jordyn got MJ strapped into her carseat. It was about an hour and a half ride to get Pauline to where she was going and Mega wanted to beat the traffic. He also had to make sure his mom was strapped and safe while he was gone. That was his biggest concern. He figured if Bossy knew where to find Pauline once, it might not have been hard for him to find her again.

"Your mom doesn't know you have a baby!" Jordyn blurted out as soon as he pulled into her driveway.

Mega instantly got nervous. He realized that in the midst of all the chaos, he hadn't even told his mom that MJ was his.

"Oh shit."

"Aw shit." Pauline said, adding on to the chain reaction.

They all just kind of sat in the car staring at each other like teenagers who were about to be in trouble. Even MJ was looking around like she was nervous.

"Well," Jordyn looked back at MJ and laughed a little. "Time to meet your new granny."

MJ smiled like she knew what Jordyn was talking about. And Mega thought she probably did, as smart as she was.

"Hey ma." He smiled nervously once she opened the door.

"Hey baby."

His mother greeted him and everyone else as she normally would. As soon as she laid her eyes on MJ, she already knew who she belonged to. She looked exactly like him when he was a baby.

"Uhh…." she said, staring directly at MJ.

Mega was speechless. He didn't even know how to break the news to her, even though he knew she already knew.

"Who's this?"

Mega looked at Jordyn for the right answer.

"I'm talking to you, Mr. Don't be looking at her." His mother said, waiting for him to open his mouth.

"That's my baby." He gulped. "Mila uh-Mila had her and hid her from me."

His mother looked like she wanted to go find Mila herself and put her foot up her ass.

"And how long have you known this and you're just now telling me? What I been telling you about that girl? From the first time you brought her over to my house I told you I didn't like her."

"I know ma," he sighed. "It's a long story that I promise I'll tell you about when we get back. Right now, we gotta go."

"Mhm." His mom rolled her eyes at him, hanging his head low. "Come on in here, Pauline. Let Mega take you over to the guest house. And how you feel about this, Ms. Jordyn?"

Jordyn's eyes got wide as saucers. She was nervous to give her an answer, but she told the truth.

"I don't like it. But, I've been dealing with it."

"Don't let no man take you for a ride. I don't care if he is my son. Now let me hold this big old baby before y'all go."

Jordyn laughed and handed her her grandbaby. She loved Mega's mom. That woman told it like it was and didn't hold her tongue for shit. She guessed she needed that kind of tough love in her life, because she felt more at peace after hearing the woman's piece of mind.

"You look just like your daddy, girl. Just like him." She pulled out her phone and pulled up a baby picture of her son to show her grand. "You see that? That's your daddy when he was about your age. Fat and sassy. You see him?"

MJ smiled, laughed and giggled at her grandma talking to her and showing her pictures.

She even leaned in to give the woman a peck on the lips. Something she learned by watching Jordyn and Mega. MJ loved her kisses and loved to give kisses.

"How you end up with this baby, miss lady?" his mom asked, while they stood at the door waiting for Mega to return.

"It's a long story." Jordyn nervously laughed.

"Well, give me the short version."

"I'm not proud to say this cause I've never been this type of girl, but Mila did something really foul to your son. I don't even know what made me go snooping on her page, but I did and found out that she had a kid. I started putting two and two together. Found out where her daycare was and paid some girls to release her to me instead. It was all for a good cause. I'll let your son tell you the rest."

She was expecting Mega's mom to start flipping out and asking questions, but she was cool about it. Jordyn figured she'd been a part of the street life before and knew how things were, so there was no need for her to ask questions.

"You must really care about my son." She gave Jordyn a motherly smile. "Only a woman in love would go to such extreme measures to protect a man."

Chapter Twenty-Two

Their flight to New York wasn't bad at all. Mega had no idea what to expect while flying with an infant, but MJ wasn't the terrible flyer. She practically slept through the entire flight. It was Jordyn who had to be calmed down and coddled like a child. She'd gone to the bathroom to throw up so many times he almost thought she wouldn't make it off the plane.

"You feel better now that we're on the ground?"

"Don't judge me. I haven't been on a plane in over ten years."

"Mhm." Mega laughed and kissed her forehead after gathering their luggage.

Although New York was one of her most favorite places to visit and she hadn't been in ages, Jordyn wasn't excited at all about their trip. She wasn't only sick to her stomach from the flight, but she was also sick from worrying about meeting up with Mila. She dreaded seeing her face to face after the way everything went down.

She was also worried about her taking MJ. Granted, Mila was still her mom, Jordyn just didn't feel like she was in the best position to care for her. She knew it would be a fight about her being overprotective, and over her being Mega's new girlfriend, so she was on edge more than he seemed to understand.

"Where's your girl?" she asked, as they made their way towards the parking garage elevators.

"She better be here. Probably the garage. Big Shaun is out there waiting on us too. Also, I need you to grab something out of the bathroom for me. Last stall. It'll be taped up under the sink."

Jordyn already knew what he needed her to get. She was nervous as hell about it, but did exactly as she was told. She knew their safety depended on it. Especially MJ's.

"Okay. Hold her. I'll be right back."

He got nervous after taking his baby. Not because he was being left alone with her, but because he wondered if Jordyn was pregnant. The thought popped into his head out of nowhere. She was back and forth to the bathroom the entire flight. MJ was loving on her more and more. There were a lot of emotions surrounding them and the thought of her being pregnant was one of them.

While he and MJ waited for Jordyn to finish up he scanned the airport. Just to be sure Mila hadn't set him up again. He thought better of the situation once he realized he was holding his baby. There was no way Mila would ever put her child in harm's way. That was what he thought, until he started to feel weird again.

There was a tall figure standing in his peripheral. Someone he didn't catch on to right away. Something in his gut told him to turn and look, but by the time he did the man had already turned his back and headed for the other direction. The build looked very familiar to Mega. The walk. The shoulders. He thought it may have been Big Shaun looking for him, but knew that wasn't the case.

An eerie feeling filled the air of the airport, making Mega clutch onto MJ a little harder. When he started to wonder what the fuck was taking Jordyn so long, she finally walked out of the bathroom.

"What's wrong?" she asked, immediately after seeing his face.

"I thought I saw somebody."

"Mila?"

"Hitman."

Jordyn felt like her skin was crawling off her bones after hearing his name. She hadn't seen her father in years after what he did to her mom and she never wanted to see him again. She wanted him dead.

"Was it him?" she asked, taking MJ into her arms for comfort. "I don't wanna see him."

Mega could feel her vibes. She was terrified of the man, and with good reason. It made him sick to think about what she'd gone through with her dad. Even sicker when he thought about what he'd done to Layton. If Mega found out that Charles was still sniffing around after him he would kill him. And Bossy.

"I don't know. Bossy was supposed to keep him on a leash after that shit with Layton. I'm starting to feel like he didn't keep his word."

"What would happen if he didn't?" she asked, already knowing the answer to her own question.

"Don't worry yourself." Mega replied, taking the diaper bag from her shoulder. "We gotta go."

After getting Mila's text, he and his duo headed for their floor in the garage. Big Shaun was already there and had eyes on Mila. He said she was alone, but didn't know that she had Charles in tow. Big Shaun already had his gun on her, so if she or anybody else made any sudden moves, it was over for them.

There was a chill in the air after they stepped off the elevator off the garage. Mega spotted Mila exactly where she said she would be and got a crazy feeling in his chest. They hadn't seen each other since the white ball and although they were in a strange place, he couldn't help but notice her beauty.

Mila had no expression on her face at all. She wanted to run over and jump into his arms like old times, but was pissed to see Jordyn there. And even more pissed that she was holding her baby. They locked eyes the entire time she headed towards them and Mega could feel the tension brewing the closer Mila got.

"Cute family." She said, as soon as she was close enough for them to hear.

"Don't start, Mila. we got more important shit to be worried about."

"Yeah," she kept her eyes fixed on Jordyn's. "We definitely do. Like why she's here in the first place."

"I'm here keeping your daughter safe." Jordyn sassed. "If it wasn't for me she would've never met her damn dad."

"If it wasn't for you she wouldn't be in this shit to begin with!"

Mila wanted to raise her fist and lash out, but quickly remembered Jordyn had MJ in her arms. Her heart sank in her chest to see her baby holding onto another woman. It hadn't been that long since she'd been away from her, but it felt like an eternity.

"Let me hold her." She said, trying her best not to cry.

Jordyn gladly wanted to hang MJ over to her, but Mega stopped her.

"Not yet. I'm not even sure I can trust you."

"Mega." She rolled her eyes. "Why the fuck would I put my own kid in danger?"

"Who knows. Look, we need to go somewhere and figure this shit out. Meet me where you said you were gonna be. And don't bring nobody with you. I'm not playing."

As soon as the words left his lips, Charles came walking up from the shadows. Mega immediately reached for his gun, but Mila jumped in front of him.

"No! He's with me."

"What the fuck!?" Mega lifted his pistol and pointed it straight at her head. "What the fuck are you doing with him?"

Mila wanted to drop dead. She couldn't believe the man she was in love with had a gun raised in her face. In front of their child. In front of his new bitch. Tears flooded her eyes as she tried to explain herself, but the rage flooding

Mega's veins wouldn't let him hear what she had to say.

"I'm not here to cause trouble." Charles said, lifting his arms to show that he was unarmed.

Big Shaun had eyes on everybody. He wanted to let shots fire, but waited until Mega gave his signal first.

"I'm here to help her."

When he heard those words he started to calm down enough to process the situation. He couldn't imagine why Charles would want to help Mila, until he thought about it. They all wanted the same thing. And that was for Bossy to be out of sight - out of mind.

"You know I should kill you, right?" Mega asked as he lowered his gun.

Charles knew how Mega was. He wasn't afraid of him, but knew that he would kill him if he made one wrong move. Aside from that, Charles couldn't get the sight of his daughter being an adult out of his head. They were standing right in front of each other and he barely even recognized her. When Mega realized they were staring at each other, he immediately ended their stand-off and got her out of there as quickly as he could.

"Meet me there." He told Mila before he, Jordyn and MJ headed to Big Shaun's truck.

They met up where Mega first laid eyes on her. It was a small cutesy restaurant right in the middle of Chinatown. Not only was the food great, but the vibe they maintained throughout the place was amazing. It was always dimly lit. fresh smelling candles and string lights hanging throughout. The feeling Mega got when they walked inside was almost unbearable for him.

"This is a cute place." Jordyn smiled. "I love this."

"Yeah." Mega agreed, remembering his first date.

Mila walked in with Charles about ten minutes after Mega was already seated. They sat at a booth in the back of the restaurant, while Mila and Charles sat up front in her favorite booth. Mega could tell she had been crying as soon as he looked at her. He felt terrible inside knowing that she was hurting, but things were very different for them.

"You okay?" he asked Jordyn while they waited for their food.

"Yes. I'm good. The vibe is a little weird, but I'm alright." She nodded.

"Okay. Just checking. I'm gonna go over here and talk to them."

"Okay. Handle your business. We'll be here."

Big Shaun sat at the table with Jordyn and MJ, while Mega made his way over to Mila and Charles. He was torn on what to do about Mila, as far as cleaning up her mess. He was torn when it came to matters of the heart too. There was still a lot of love for her lingering around, but he also had a lot of love for Jordyn. Hurting either one of them would kill him. Especially if it were Jordyn.

"I wanna get right down to business." He said, taking a seat next to Mila in the booth. "I don't trust either one of you and that should be respected. I need to know what's what. Who's after who and what y'all plan on doing about it. There's a lot of unfinished business between the three of us, but I'm willing to work together until we get Bossy out of the picture. We already know he won't accept a payoff because I won't work for him, so that leaves only one option. I don't feel like anyone at this table will disagree with it. And if so there ain't no reason for us to be talking. Agreed?"

"Agreed." Charles said.

"Yeah." Mila nodded.

She couldn't help but stare at Jordyn from across the room. The way MJ interacted with her was hard to watch. Taking care of business should've been at the forefront of Mila's mind, she just couldn't stomach the thought of her man moving on and having to share her kid with another woman.

"So, is this something serious between you two?" she asked, keeping her eyes on Jordyn and her baby.

"What?" Mega's face scrunched up.

"You and Jordyn. Is she someone you plan on keeping around? I need to know who will be in my child's life."

"That's really all you're thinking about right now? Seriously? You got your stupid ass in some real shit and you thinking about another female? Typical."

Jordyn saw the conversation between them getting heated and already knew what it was about. She tried her best not to look in their direcion, but she was worried about her man.

"He's right." Charles cut in. "There's no time for that. Bossy gave me three days to find Mila and that time is running out. He'll have somebody out to find us both real soon."

Mega thought about what he said and wondered why he didn't just kill her. That would've saved his life because he had no real use for her. To Mega, that only meant one thing. Charles wasn't only looking for her, he was also looking for him too. The hitman knew that if he found her he could use her to get to him. His recognition put Bossy, and Charles, in an even deeper hole with him. He was going to kill them both. As soon as the time was right.

"I think I may have a plan." He said, keeping his eyes locked on Charles. "I'll get up with y'all in the morning to talk about it. I gotta get the kid to bed."

Chapter Twenty-Three

Watching Mega walk away from the table was one of the most painful things Mila had ever dealt with. She was mad at herself for the decisions she made, though she felt like the love they had could outweigh anything. She missed her baby. She missed her man. She missed her old life. It pained her to think about never being able to have those things again.

"Mega, wait!" she shot up from the booth.

As she approached him his heart started to pound in his chest. He thought she might try to kiss him, or confess her dying love for him, but she wanted something else. She wanted to hold her baby. In case it was the last chance she had to do so.

"I need to hold her." She said, with tears in her eyes.

The pain Mega knew she felt hurt him as well. He wanted to say no. He wanted to keep MJ as far away from their situation as possible, but his heart wouldn't let him turn away from her pain. MJ needed to know that her mother was still around.

"Okay." He nodded. "I'll get her."

She anxiously waited for him to return with their child. It was the first time her heart felt any kind of happiness since the ball. Especially seeing him hold her and the way her little hands played with the necklace on his neck.

"Hey mamas." She sobbed as soon as her daughter touched her arms. "My baby."

MJ recognized her immediately. She giggled and jibber-jabbered while Mega stood back watching. He smiled a little, watching his daughter and the mother of his child, wishing that things could be different. Unfortunately, he didn't feel like they would ever be the same.

"Let's step outside for a minute."

Jordyn was hanging onto the edge of her seat when she saw them exit the restaurant together. For some reason she got the feeling that they would sneak away to run off into the sunset or something, and it really hurt her feelings. Although she knew there were things Mega needed to clear up with Mila in private, the thought of him talking to his ex was hard to cope with.

"Thank you." Mila said, once they were in private.

"For what?"

"Letting me hold her. Taking care of her through all of this. Not killing me after finding out she was yours. I don't know. Everything."

"Yeah." He nodded. "We have to figure this out for her. I wasn't happy at all when I found out, but she grew on me."

"She likes you." Mila smiled.

Hearing her say that made him feel better about being a father. He was scared as hell to be a parent and he didn't know why. There had never been a time where he and Mila couldn't figure things out. He knew being parents would be no different.

"I'm scared." She said, giving him a look he couldn't turn away from. "What if I don't make it out of this? What's gonna happen to MJ?"

"Don't talk like that. You gon be alright. I'ma take care of it. MJ won't have to worry about none of that. She'll grow up with both of her parents and have a good life."

Mila hung onto his every word. He had never failed to come through for her before, so she believed everything would be alright. She had no idea what would come of them after the smoke cleared, but there was hope for her to still be alive and that was enough for her at that moment.

"How are we gonna do visitation once this is over?" he asked, making sure to be clear in his requests. "I wanna be present in her life. I'm not some deadbeat dad who doesn't care to have his kid around. I actually wanna be there. I wanna experience things with her and she needs a father."

"I know. I'm sorry I kept her away from you for as long as I did. That wasn't fair to either of you. She's your daughter and you can see her whenever you want. I have no problem with that."

Their talk was easier than he thought it would be. It felt good to be able to have a civilized conversation with her. No yelling. Screaming. Fighting. Just a real grown-up conversation that brought them a step closer to results.

"I'll call you in the morning. I gotta get her to bed and you need to lay low. Where you staying tonight?"

"I'm going back to Philly. I been staying in some shitty ass hotel out there. I knew I couldn't stay in the city for too long because they know I'm from here. So." She shrugged. "You and Charles are the only ones who know where I'm at."

"Yeah, well don't be too trusting of him. Something ain't right about that nigga. I'll follow you out to Philly and get a room out there. I'll get you hooked up where I'm at so you don't have to be too far."

"Thank you."

On the inside of the restaurant, Charles slowly made his way over to the table where Jordyn sat. She watched him with a hawk's eye as he approached. Big Shaun too. He didn't know Jordyn from a hole in the wall, but she meant something to Mega so he was prepared to protect that at all cost.

"I don't want any trouble." Charles said, keeping his voice as light as he knew how. "I just wanna have a word. If that's okay."

For a moment, Jordyn stared at him wondering where he got the nerve. But, there was something softer in his eyes that day. She figured it was the removal of drugs from his life and that made her want to hear what he had to say.

"That's fine." She said, sitting up straight in her chair.

Charles didn't know where to start. He was amazed at how much older she looked. The last time he'd seen her she was just a baby.

"Wo." He chuckled. "I just can't get over how much different you look. The last time I saw you…."

"You tried to kill my mother." She cut him off. "That was the last time you saw me."

Embarrassment washed over The Hitman's face as flashbacks from that gory night played like a movie in his mind. He could imagine the hate and disgust his daughter had for him, and she had every reason to hate him. He was a piece of shit father who tried to take away the only person that loved her. There was no forgiveness in that.

"There are no amount of words that can express the regret I live with everyday." He confessed. "I won't sit here and make any excuses for myself. What I did was wrong. I don't expect you, or your mother, to ever forgive me and I thank you for letting me get that off my chest."

Jordyn was speechless. She wasn't expecting him to be so transparent with his emotions. She didn't even know whether or not she could trust what he said, but something in her softened towards him after hearing him out. She remembered a time where he wasn't all that bad. If it weren't for the drugs, Jordyn felt like Charles could have been a better father. There was just so much damage done it was hard to come back from.

When Mega turned and saw Charles sitting at the table he was shook. His first instinct was to rush inside and remove Jordyn from the situation. But with a single look, she stopped him before he could. Mila saw him go into protective mode and felt like all hope for them was lost. He loved Jordyn. She knew it. It was written all over his face.

"I think we should get out of here. We've been here too long."

"Yeah." He nodded. Keeping his eyes on Jordyn. "It's time to get MJ to bed. It's late."

Jordyn was quiet on the ride to Philly. A lot of thoughts and childhood memories were on her mind and she needed time to process it. She didn't know why she felt softer towards her father. Or why she referred to him as her father in the first place. She hated him for what he'd done to her mother and for some reason, that hate was slowly fading away.

"You okay?" Mega asked, placing a hand on her thigh.

"Somewhat." She sighed and rested her head on his shoulder.

"Anything I can do?"

"No. I just have a lot on my mind and feel a little emotional."

He understood that and didn't pressure her to talk. He figured whenever she was ready to speak about it, she would. There was a little bit of worry about what she and Charles spoke about, but he knew it couldn't have been anything to worry about because Big Shaun hadn't said anything.

The two hour ride to Philly was tiring. Jordyn and MJ were asleep by the time they arrived and Mega was ready for bed himself. He booked three rooms that night. One for them. One for Big Shaun. And one for Mila. Charles said he had a place secured not too far from them and that was fine for Mega. He really didn't care where Charles stayed as long as he stayed in his lane.

After showering and winding down for the night, Mega poured himself a drink and stepped out on the balcony to smoke a blunt. He also wanted to give Jordyn some time to herself to gather her feelings. However, instead of going straight to bed she joined him on the balcony.

"What you doing up?" he asked, maneuvering a chair for her to sit down.

"I don't know. What you doing up?"

"Just thinking."

So was she. Jordyn thought about a lot of things. Her emotions were unusually high during that time and she had no idea why. All she knew was that she wanted Mega to hurry up and clear shit up for Mila, so they could finally start a real relationship.

"Charles apologized to me tonight. I don't know how to feel about it."

Mega was shocked. "Oh yeah?"

"Yeah. He said he's been living with so much regret all these years. I don't know if I really believe him though. Something in me does, but something else tells me I'm way past forgiveness."

"You don't have to forgive him just because he's your dad. Sometimes we tend to forget that it's okay to remove toxic people from your life. No matter who it is."

"Do you feel that way about Mila?"

That was a hard question for him to answer. His silence immediately made Jordyn want to get on a flight back to Miami, but she waited to hear what he had to say before jumping to conclusions.

"Mila and I had a serious talk about MJ. There's still more to be talked about, but it was a good talk. It's hard for me to forgive her completely, but I think with time it might be possible. At least for the sake of co-parenting."

"Good." Jordyn nodded. "That's good. I'm happy for y'all."

Mega could sense her doubt as soon as she spoke. She was worried about him rekindling a relationship with Mila. Something he understood from her standpoint. Although he felt like he loved Jordyn, he wasn't 100% sure what would happen between him and the mother of his child, so she had every right to feel doubtful.

Chapter Twenty-Four

When Mega's phone rang at 9:00 that morning he was pissed. He didn't go to bed until after 6 a.m and was one cranky man if woken up before his alarm. The number was unknown and had called him three times already. On the fourth call he jumped up to answer, thinking it might have been Mila.

"Who is this?" he answered, sleep still in his voice.

"The man you've been avoiding. How are you?"

It took a moment for him to recognize the voice, but when he did he was kind of glad he answered the phone.

"Bossy, the man in charge." He laughed a little. "How can I be of service to you this morning?"

"I'm in Philadelphia and I want to set up a time for our meeting." Bossy said, sounding friendly. "You're a hard man to track down, Mr. Navarro."

"That's because I have no desire to be tracked down. I've declined your business offer several times, so I'm not sure where the confusion lies."

Bossy's blood turned cold. If there was one thing he hated to hear, it was the word "no". No one ever told him no and if they did, he always made them reconsider.

"I just want to meet with you. We can go over what I have to offer and if it's still a no." He paused to think of another way to say he wouldn't accept no for an answer. "Then I will ask you again another day."

"And everyday I will tell you no. I'm not interested in doing business with you. I do have something else I want to talk to you about though, while we're on the phone."

"Anything." Bossy flirted.

"I want Mila's name off your list. Whatever she owes you I will triple. And I'll even let Charles live."

Bossy laughed uncontrollably at the mention of Charles. He had no more use for Charles after he told him where Mega was. He had planned on killing him anyway.

"I have no use for Charles. You should have killed him a long time ago. Your girlfriend however, we may be able to work something out."

"This is exactly why we can't do business. You're untrustworthy."

Mega hung up the phone and immediately dialed Mila. Bossy was in Philly and there was only one way he would've known where to find him.

"I need to see you. Now. meet me in the stairwell."

"I'm coming."

Mila grew nervous. She went to bed with a weird feeling that night and dreaded waking up to whatever it was Mega needed to see her about. It wasn't anything good, she knew that just by the tone of his voice. Her hands began to tremble as she reached for the door of the stairwell and before she could grab it, Mega yanked it open and pulled her inside.

"What the fuck is going on?" she asked, scared to death.

"Mila, don't play with me. What the fuck do you and Charles have going on? I'm sick of the shit. I don't wanna kill you, but I swear to God I will end your shit right now. Start talking."

The two of them had been in several fights over the years, so she was used to him raising his voice at her. What she wasn't used to was the violence and rage behind it.

"We don't have anything going on! What the fuck?" she frowned. "He came to me saying he could help because he has his own shit going on with whoever this guy is. That's it!"

Mega was furious. He didn't know whether to believe her or not and that infuriated him even more. Not being able to trust her made him want to leave her to fend for herself.

"I just got a call from the guy and he's here."

"Shit!" She began to tremble. "How did he find us?"

"Exactly."

"I didn't tell him! Why would I tell him where I am? Or you! You have my kid!"

What she said made sense to him a little. But then he thought, what if she told Bossy where he was to clear her own name. Afterall, Bossy wanted Mega more than he did her, so that made sense too.

"Mega, I know what I did was fucked up and I'm sorry I got us into this shit, but you have to believe me. I did not tell this man where to find us. It had to be Charles. Had to be. And even that doesn't make any sense because he said the man was gon kill kim anyway. It didn't matter whether he knew where you were or not. That was the whole reason he stepped to me the way he did."

"He got spooked and tried to cut a deal thinking I would give in to Bossy and his demands. That nigga don't know me too well."

"What does he want with you?"

"The motherfucker wants me to push work for him."

"Why don't you? Ain't that what you do anyway?"

"It is. But not for niggas like that. Niggas like that'll get you killed."

Mila already knew how he was when it came to business. Mega was real lowkey and ran a tight ship. Bossy was flashy and wanted everybody to know exactly who he was. Mega wasn't like that. He was a classy businessman. Very subtle. Not only that, but he was a made-man. He built his empire from the ground up on his own, so working for another man would never be an option for Mega.

"What's the move?" Mila asked. "I see your wheels spinning."

He stared at her for a moment, really contemplating on their trust issues. Deep down inside he knew Mila was a rider. She made a fucked up decision that she didn't think would go as far as it did, but she was really down for Mega. If he asked her to kill somebody she would. No questions asked.

"You really down with this gangster shit." He said, giving her props.

"You put me on and I ain't been the same since."

"That's what's up. First things first, I'm sending MJ and Jordyn back to Florida. I know you might not like that, but that's the safest place for her to be right now."

"No," Mila nodded. "I agree. They both need to be kept safe. I was thinking about that last night. Jordyn and I might not see eye to eye as women, but she's definitely good for MJ. I appreciate her for standing in when I couldn't. My daughter means the world to me and she held it down, for real. I give her mad props."

Her speech came as a shock to Mega. He wasn't expecting Mila to ever come around to the thought of Jordyn being in MJ's life, but he was happy that she opened up to it. It made things lighter for him.

"Cool. Then we gotta take care of Charles. Don't say shit to him about me knowing Bossy's in town. Make him think you're on his side, or you don't know nothing. Whatever to get him off somewhere alone tonight, then that nigga's good as dead."

"What about your girl? You don't think she'll feel a way about you killing her dad?"

"That's just gon have to be something she deals with. He spoke his peace to her last night, so that's good enough. That nigga gotta go. She knew that after what he did to Layton. I was just waiting for the right time to do it. And that's tonight."

He thought about telling Jordyn his plans for Charles, but figured it'd be best if he didn't. She was already going through whatever emotional turmoil she was going through, and he didn't want to make it any worse. If she found out Charles was dead he would help her through it. And if she didn't, maybe she would think he continued on with life living in his regrets. Either way, Charles was a done deal.

"What about Bossy? How we gon get to him?"

"Charles. Get him to meet tonight to talk about this deal with Bossy. He'll think I'm actually considering it and tell Bossy where we are to save himself. Once he drops that location I'ma smoke his ass."

"Sounds like a plan."

Mila was down for whatever, no matter how big the risk was. She just wanted the shit to be done and over with so she could move on with her life and raise her daughter.

"Come to the room so you can see MJ before they head out. I'm bout to book their flights now."

It had been a while since Mila had been able to see her baby first thing in the morning. She missed waking up to her smiling face waiting for her cereal. She missed the slobbery kisses she planted on her cheeks as she tried to wake her mama. Mila missed being around MJ period. She'd never gone a single day away from her, so their time spent apart was definitely a huge adjustment.

When they returned to Mega's room, Jordyn was up in the kitchen making MJ breakfast. The moment she saw Mila walk in behind him her heart nearly stopped. She wasn't afraid of Mila, her presence was just unexpected.

"I'm sending y'all back to Florida today. My mom is gonna get y'all from the airport."

"Why? What's going on?" Jordyn grew nervous.

"Bossy's here."

Jordyn was confused at how he found out where they were. Her first mind said that Mila had another trick up her sleeve, but she didn't know what to truly believe at that point. Until Mila asked her if they could have a moment alone to talk.

"I'm gonna go book the tickets and start packing."

He left MJ with Mila, who was more than happy to see her, and gave the women their privacy to clear the air.

"Morning." Mila said, trying to start the conversation off on a good foot.

"Morning." Jordyn replied, already on edge.

"Look, I'm not really good at apologies, but I do owe you one. I don't wanna beat around the bush or anything, so I'm gonna get straight to it."

Jordyn was surprised Mila gave her that much, so she knew whatever else she had to say would leave her in shock.

"I didn't like what you did, but now that I look back it was for the best. I know we don't see eye to eye as women, but I do appreciate what you did for my daughter."

Mila left the ball in Jordyn's court. It was hard for her to apologize when she was wrong, and even harder for her to be cordial with someone she looked at like an enemy. When she thought about it, she really didn't see Jordyn as her enemy. She was just jealous that her man had moved on to another female. That was a hard pill for her to swallow.

"Well," Jordyn said, stepping from behind the counter to shake Mila's hand. "I appreciate that. I'm not proud of what I did either, but I'm happy that I did it. And we don't have to be mean girls to each other. I don't have any beef with you, I just want this shit done and over with so we can figure out our next moves in life. This baby deserves a happy life. She's such a sweet girl."

It took a lot, but Mila put her pride aside and accepted Jordyn's hand. She wasn't bad at all. In fact, Mila felt like Jordyn was someone she could actually be friends with in different circumstances. She didn't know for sure, but she was open to figuring it out.

Chapter Twenty-Five

Mila waited in the living room of Mega's suite with their baby, while he had a word with Jordyn in the bedroom. She was scared. Scared for him. Scared for Mila. Scared for MJ. Most of all, she was scared of how she'd look if anything happened to them and she had to take care of their baby. She felt stupid, but figured that was what love made a person do. She witnessed it between her own mother and father.

However, Jordyn wanted more out of love. She didn't want to be tied down to a man who could go back to his ex at any given moment. And she definitely didn't want to waste her time caring for someone else's kid when she hadn't even had her own yet. A lot of things ran through her mind that day, but only one thing remained the same and that was her love and loyalty to Mega.

"What's gonna happen for us once this is over?" she asked, as she got dressed to head for the airport. "I don't wanna be a bitch and start a fight or nothing, but I don't wanna be doing all of this for nothing either."

"What you mean? Once this is over we can keep doing what we been doing."

"And what has that been?"

When he thought about it, they really hadn't been doing anything. He'd been on the go everyday since they got together, so they hadn't even spent any real time with each other. Mega knew in his heart that he loved Jordyn, he just didn't know how to be done with Mila completely. And that got in the way of his feelings for her.

"You wanna be with me?" He asked, stepping into her path in the bathroom.

"Obviously. I just don't know if you really wanna be with me. I mean, I know you like me? But, I'm not sure how far that will go."

In that moment, Mega felt the need to be completely transparent with Jordyn, he just couldn't. He wanted to figure things out on his own. When it came to Mila, there couldn't be any other influences. If there was, he was afraid he might stray right back to her and that wasn't what he wanted. He just needed to figure out how to let her go.

"I wanna be with you."

It was crazy how he could be so short and nonchalant with Jordyn and she still loved him. She still wanted to be with him. Still craved his affection. She reminded herself to stay patient with him, because he really was a good guy. She just felt like she'd caught him at a bad time and maybe they wouldn't work out.

"I feel like all this shit going on is making you emotional." He said, while pulling her in for a hug. "Either that or you pregnant."

He said it as a joke, but it quickly made Jordyn realize that she hadn't had a period in a while. Her mind tried to tell her it was late because of stress, but there were times where she was more stressed than she was and still had a period.

"Uhhh...."

Mega's heart dropped to his balls. He hadn't heard her talk about having a period either, but she was eating more. Being emotional. And she was sick on the plane.

"Uhhh what?"

"What if I'm pregnant?" She grew nervous. "Oh my god. What if I'm pregnant?"

That time she was asking herself. She pushed away from Mega, sat down on the toilet and let her head fall into her hands to cry. Being pregnant was a scary thought for Jordyn. She wanted to be established before she went that far with her life. Not lugging around her boyfriend's baby mama's baby. Or taking trips out of state to run away from people trying to kill her. That wasn't the life she wanted for herself, or for her kid.

"Are you pregnant?"

"I don't know. With all this shit going on I haven't even had the time to think about that."

"Shit." He kneeled down in front of her. "I'm gonna be a dad again."

She couldn't help but laugh at that. He sounded like a child who was afraid, but more than ready to step up. That made her feel better about the possibility, even though she hoped she wasn't. Not because she didn't see herself having kids with Mega, but because she wasn't ready. She didn't think he was ready either. And again, she found herself coddling him, instead of taking the time to truly process what she was doing with her own life.

"I don't know." She sighed and kissed his lips. "Let's go. I'll take a test when I get back and let you know for sure."

"You don't wanna do it now?"

"We don't have time now. And no, I don't. I'm not ready to know yet myself."

"Okay. I respect that."

When they exited the room, Mila had MJ dressed, fed, and ready to go. She wasn't ready to send her baby away again, but she had to do what she had to do. When she looked at Jordyn she could tell she had been crying, and Mila felt bad for her. The shit going on between her and Mega would've never been accepted by her. She gave it to Jordyn though, the girl held him down like no other.

"You riding?" he asked Mila, before they walked out the door.

"Uh, yeah. If that's cool with y'all."

"Yeah that's cool." Jordyn chimed in. "She needs to see MJ before whatever happens happens."

Jordyn was right. They didn't know how their plan was going to play out for sure. Graves and prison were very real, and a definite possibility for the both of them if shit didn't go as planned. Mila was so anxious to get it over with that she hadn't taken the time to think about that.

"Yeah." Mila nodded, feeling even more anxious. "Jordyn's right. Thank you for that."

"No problem. Now let's go so we can get this shit over with."

Something about the way she said that turned Mega on. She sounded like she was the one calling the shots and sending them on a mission, instead of the other way around. He liked that. She sounded like a GANGSTA. Mila too. It made her feel like Jordyn would do anything to protect her daughter. And she was right.

Big Shaun had a car waiting for Mega in the garage of the hotel. He felt like it would be best if he drove around in something different, just to be on the safe side when it came to Charles. He'd also been looking for Charles ever since Mega told him Bossy was in town. He figured if he got to him first he could track down Bossy himself and save Mega some trouble.

Mega knew better than that. Bossy was planning to kill Charles himself, so naturally Charles would want to stay as far away from him as he could. At least, until he knew for sure his life would be spared. However, the one thing Bossy always kept his word about was killing.

The airport was packed as usual. It was risky business for them to be out and about, so Mega wanted to get Jordyn and MJ on their plane as quickly as possible. Big Shaun had a friend who worked on the runway tossing bags and checking tires, and paid him to do a sweep of the plane to make sure none of Bossy's men were there waiting for them to board. Mega paid off one of the boarding agents to give him a list of names of the people on the flight, and once everything checked out he was ready for them to get going.

"Are you gonna be okay?" Jordyn asked while she hugged him.

"I plan to be."

"I'm serious. This ain't a game Mega. I don't want anything to happen to you."

Mila loved on MJ at the boarding gate while Mega held onto Jordyn. She did her best not to focus on the love he showed Jordyn, and to be happy for them, but there was a streak of jealousy rising in her heart. It wasn't something she wanted to feel intentionally, she just remembered all the times he showed her the same love. It hurt to lose that.

"Alright, y'all gotta get out of here." He said, kissing her lips. "Call me as soon as you land."

"I will. I promise. Y'all be careful, please."

Instead of handing MJ over to Jordyn, Mila gave her to Mega and quickly pulled Jordyn in for a hug. It came as a surprise to all of them because there was so much bad blood, but her hug felt genuine. Jordyn hugged her back like they had been friends all their lives. She couldn't imagine how scared Mila was, but she could feel it in that hug.

"I'm sorry," Mila said, still hugging her. "You're just so motherly I felt like I needed that. Since, you know."

"I know. You don't have to say it." Jordyn replied and tightened her grip. "Be careful, okay?"

"I'm trying."

"Don't worry about MJ. I'll make sure she's straight."

"Thank you."

While Mila and Jordyn shared their hug, Mega took the time to hug and kiss MJ. She reached out for her mama and it almost made him cry. He knew he had to get Mila out of her shit and back home to their child, otherwise he'd have a hard time raising her. Not because he didn't know how to, but the pain he would feel for MJ would be unbearable.

Once Jordyn and MJ boarded their plane, Mega and Mila stood at the window and watched them take off. She never imagined a life where they weren't together. Especially after having a child by him. She certainly didn't imagine herself being cordial with any other woman he decided to date after her. Yet alone send her child to another state with the woman. A lot of things had changed for Mila during the time she spent away from her baby. A lot of scary things, but what she got out of those things were essential to her growth as a woman. And a mother.

"Jordyn's not so bad." She admitted, as they left the airport.

"Yeah, she's cool." Mega smiled a little.

"It's okay to love her, you know? I'll get over it."

He was shocked to hear Mila talk that way. He thought she would be mad at him for the rest of their lives if he ever decided to move on for good.

"Will you really?"

"I will." She nodded. "I'll be sad for a while, but I took a lot away from our relationship. A lot of things that will continue to help me grow. I appreciate you for that even if we don't work out."

"That's big of you. I thought we would have beef forever. Just don't have none of these crazy niggas around my daughter."

"Mega," she laughed and rolled her eyes. "I won't."

Chapter Twenty-Six

After leaving the airport, Mega went back to their hotel so he and Mila could pack and possibly head back to New york. Before leaving, they ordered some takeout and sat down to rehearse their plan. He needed Mila to be on point when it came to playing her role, otherwise their plan wasn't going to work and she could end up dead.

"Where you plan on meeting up with Charles?"

"He wants to meet somewhere out here. I told him I was going back to New York tonight to get the money for him to return."

"The money?" Mega frowned, not knowing what she was talking about.

"That $250,000 I got off Polo. I still have it. Charles fed me some bullshit about him being able to return it and clear my name. Of course I know he probably plans on taking the money and dipping, but whatever."

Mega had forgotten all about the money she skipped town with. Hearing that she still had it changed the game entirely. He couldn't send her to meet Charles alone. Especially with that kind of money on her. He knew the second

Charles laid eyes on that money, he might kill Mila and be out. That was just the kind of grimey nigga that he was.

"Change of plans then." He stood up and paced the floor of the living room. "You gotta meet Charles early. I'll tell Bossy he can meet me in New York by midnight. We meet up with Charles, do what you gotta do to get that location. I'll creep up and take the nigga out and hit Bossy before he gets on the road to New York. If I know a crazy motherfucker like Bossy, he wants his money plus some. Charles ain't that stupid to run off with his money. He knows he'll have niggas on his head before he can even blink."

"Makes sense." Mila nodded. "You make the shit sound so easy."

"It will be if we stick to the plan. Charles won't know I'm there. Try to get the nigga to meet off somewhere lowkey. I know he has to have his man's location somewhere in his phone. How else are they gon meet up for him to exchange the money?"

Time seemed to fly by while they waited for their meet up with Charles. As the clock ticked closer and closer, Mila grew more nervous. Her heart was racing, her palms started to sweat. She even felt like she would throw up at one point. Mega was cool, calm, and collected. He was used to doing crime and taking lives. It was a way of life for him, but for her the shit didn't come so easy.

"You wanna hit this blunt?" he asked, as he cruised towards their destination.

"Yes, oh my god. My nerves are shot right now."

"I can tell." He laughed. "Just chill, you gon be alright. That nigga ain't gon make no move until he get that money."

"What if he gets mad or some shit when he sees I only brought ten grand?"

"Tell him you had to make sure he wasn't setting you up. Shit, he'll understand that. Small talk with him first, see if he'll tell you where he's supposed to take the money."

Mila was good at small talk. That was one of her specialties. Especially when it came to men. Niggas were always trying to get at her, it didn't matter how old they were. As soon as they laid eyes on her it was like they turned stupid. Mega was the only one ever able to give her a run for her money. That was why she loved him the way that she did.

Before getting to their destination, Mega made her drop him off a few blocks away. Just so Charles wouldn't get spooked and flee the scene.

He had his own car waiting, and told Mila as soon as she got the address for the money drop, send him a text to let him know.

"Remember, play it cool." He said, getting out to switch cars.

"What if I can't get the address from him?"

"You got this, Mila. You'll get it. Now let's go so we can be done with this shit."

Once Mega was out of the car, Mila took a deep breath to get herself together. She knew she had to get the information they needed for the sake of her daughter. She wasn't ready to die and leave her kid without a mother. She had to get it.

She saw Charles waiting by the water as she pulled into the secluded park he suggested. It was dark and chilly that night. Not only because the air was crisp, but also because of the circumstances. She didn't trust Charles, no matter how friendly he tried to be with her. He'd already crossed the line by telling his boss where to find Mega, so there was no telling what else he might do.

Charles turned around when he saw the car pull in behind him. The park he chose was supposed to have been abandoned, but niggas went out there to make drops and get high all the time. That was why he chose it. No one would know where to look for her body once he killed her. He made a deal with Bossy to get his money back in blood and his life would be spared.

Once Mila was dead and gone, Mega would come after him, and Bossy would keep him protected. That was the plan he discussed and though he had a feeling Bossy was playing him, Charles vowed to keep his word anyway. All for the love of the money.

"I almost thought you wouldn't show up." He said, as she walked towards the docks. "You have trouble finding the park?"

His voice sent a slight shiver down Mila's spine. The way it bounced off the cool darkness of the night didn't sit right with her. He sounded like a cold-blooded murderer.

"Nah. The traffic started to pick up." She said.

She was dressed down in a form fitting jogging suit and a pair of vans, just in case she had to run. Her curves were curving and her hair was waving against the chilly breeze coming off the water, making Charles see something other than the money he was after. She was light years younger than he was, but that never stopped him from shooting his shot with a hottie.

"You bring the money?"

"Why else would I come here?" she asked, trying to sound as polite as possible.

"Okay." He chuckled. "Where is it?"

"It's in the trunk. But, how do I know you ain't just playing with me? How do I know you won't kill me as soon as I hand over the money? I don't trust shit in this game. Especially a man."

"And you shouldn't. Men have a crazy way about them when it comes to women and money."

Charles inched closer to her with an evil look in his eyes. He knew once he got his hands on Mila there would be no fight. He was way stronger than she was. The only issue he had was he couldn't keep his eyes off her curves long enough to figure out which way he wanted to grab her.

"So I guess that means you are planning to kill me?"

"I didn't say that."

Mega started to get a bad feeling while he waited for Mila to give him the word. He felt like their plan wasn't going to work and it was stupid to send her to meet Charles alone. So, instead of waiting for her to send him a signal, he drove a block away from the park and walked the rest of the way to finish the job himself.

He came in from the back of the park and could see Mila inching her way towards the water as Charles slowly got closer to her. Mega could hear muffled voices that became more clear the closer he got. Charles wanted more than just the money from Mila. He wanted something Mega knew she would never give up. Not to a man like Charles, anyway.

"Where's Bossy? I'll give him the money myself." She said, fear rattling her voice.

"That's not the plan." Charles chuckled. "That motherfucker was planning to kill me anyway. I'm sure he's at the grand casino eating some fancy steak. Drinking some fancy wine. Shitting on the little man like he's better than everybody. He thinks I'm gonna come back and give him $250,000 and just wait for him to kill me? He's gotta be one of the stupidest motherfuckers I know." He leaned back and let out a hefty laugh.

Mega knew exactly where Bossy was. The same grand casino that he made some of his weakest business plays at. It was the only spot in Philly where wannabe gangsters went to make themselves feel special. It was no wonder Bossy would post up in a place like that.

"You've always been a stupid motherfucker yourself." Mega said, as he stepped from the darkness onto the dock.

The second Mila heard his vice her heart began to flutter. She thought she was as good as dead, but Mega always came through. She didn't even get the chance to make it to her phone and there he was to save her ass once again.

"Turn around nigga."

When Charles turned around and stared directly down the barrel of a gun, he knew his life was over.

"Yeah." Mega said, pointing the barrel square in the middle of the big man's head. "Niggas get quiet when the script is flipped. You really thought you would have one up on me for the rest of your life, didn't you?"

Charles kept his mouth shut. He was already a dead man, so there was no sense in him begging for his life.

"Do it." He stepped in closer. "End it all right now. If you have the…."

Before he could even get the word out of his mouth, Mega pulled the trigger. Charles hit the ground like a sack of potatoes, while Mega stood over his body admiring his kill. Mila was ready to get the fuck out of dodge before anyone came, so she snapped Mega out of his trance as she started to look for Charles' cellphone.

"What are you doing? Don't touch him."

"Don't you need his phone to figure out where Bossy is?"

"I know where he is."

The look in Mega's eyes scared her a little. He looked like he was about to go on a full blown killing spree. She was afraid to ask him what his next moves were, and she didn't have to. He told her.

"I got you a ticket to go back home. You need to get to the airport now."

"What about the money?"

"Take it with you. I'll have somebody at the gate to let you through with it."

"No, Mega. What are you gonna do? I'm not leaving you." She frantically shook her head.

"Mila, you have to go home and be with MJ. I can take care of the rest of this shit. I'll fly out right behind you."

As much as she pleaded with him to let her wait for him, he wasn't having it. Mega knew there would be bloodshed after his meeting with Bossy and he didn't want Mila being caught in the crossfire. If he ended up dying that night, at least one of them had to be there for their daughter.

"Promise me you'll get on that plane." He said, as she drove him back to his car.

"I don't wanna make a promise I don't know if I can keep."

Chapter Twenty-Seven

On her way to the airport, Mila decided to drive by the casino first, just to check it out. She had a few hours to kill before her flight back to Miami, but still went back and forth with herself on whether or not she would leave. When she drove by the casino the first time, she didn't see anyone out of the ordinary. Then again, she had never seen the man in question before, so she didn't really know who to look for.

It wasn't until her third time around she saw someone who looked dangerous. She knew right away it was Bossy because she remembered Mega saying the guy was a flamboyant gay. And also because of all the men in black suits he had surrounding him. Bossy and his entire entourage were manning down the back of the casino.

Mila knew there was no way in hell Mega could walk in there alone and turn down a deal. Even if he had Big Shaun with him they still wouldn't have enough for all the men she saw.

She thought about calling him to tell him she wasn't leaving and that she had a plan, but knew he would only try and talk her out of it. So, she scratched that out and reached out to a nigga she knew could help.

"Hello, who this?"

"This Rudy?"

"Depends on who's asking."

"It's Mila. Your sister."

Rudy was a hot headed nigga that Mila found out was her brother a few years ago. Her father stepped out on her mom when she was a kid and after finding out that he got some woman pregnant, she took Mila and left. Her dad was always reaching out to them wanting to know where they were. He also wanted Mila to get to know her brother. For a long time she was bitter about having a sibling, but when she finally bumped into Rudy on a trip back home, they quickly became inseparable.

"Oh shit! What's up sis? You in town?"

"I'm over in Philly. Listen, I can't go into too much detail over the phone, but I need your help. I'm willing to pay for it too. You think you can gang up some niggas and get out here tonight?"

"How many?"

"A lot."

"Send me the addy and I got you."

"Bet."

Rudy was a real street nigga who was all about the street life. He knew Mega before he knew Mila and was always trying to get down with him, but Mega would never put him on because he was too young. He was also too wild. The type of shit Rudy was into wasn't Mega's speed. Rudy was loud and obnoxious with his shit. It wasn't until he got sentenced to a seven year bid that he calmed his ass down.

when he got home was when he met Mila. He thought she was just some random chick from around the way and tried to spit game to her, but a familiar face let him know who she was. When he found out they had the same father, they started to bond over old stories and sparked up a real relationship. She had his back whenever he needed something and vice versa. Especially when it had something to do with criminal activity.

After sending Rudy the address where they were going to meet up, Mila went back to the hotel to get her head together. She sat in the parking lot to make sure she didn't run into Mega and got her head in the game to come up with a plan. However, nothing good came to mind. Mega was meeting Bossy in a classy casino full of people. There was no way a bunch of niggas from the hood could walk into a place like that without setting off alarms. She didn't want any innocent bystanders getting hurt, nor did she want to get picked off by the police.

Whatever they did had to be done with class. And it had to be done discreetly as well. She thought about calling her mom to get some insight, but she had never been good at planning shit either. Anything Brenda ever did was done off a wing and a prayer.

"Fuck." She cursed herself for not being able to think. "Who the fuck can I call about this?"

She sat in the car for another ten minutes before an unexpected person popped into her mind. Someone she would have never thought to ask for help with something so mischievous. Even though they had done some creep shit themselves once upon a time.

"Hey, what's up?"

"Jordyn, I need your help."

That was all Jordyn needed to hear before her heart nearly ran out of her chest. She thought for sure Mila was going to tell her Mega was dead or in jail. The lump that grew in her throat was so huge it prevented her from talking.

"Mega's fine. Right now, anyway. He wanted me to get on a plane and come back to Miami, but I had a bad feeling about leaving him. He's planning to meet Bossy at the grand casino and I really don't think he's gonna make it out of there after declining whatever offer he keeps declining. Even if he has Big Shaun with him," she shook her head. "I just don't know what to do. But, I can't leave him."

Jordyn let out a huge sigh of relief. Her heart was still pounding in her chest, but she was more calm than she was at the sight of the call. It actually surprised her that Mila called and asked for her help. Especially when it came down to Mega.

"Where is he now?"

"Upstairs in his room. He's supposed to meet with Bossy at midnight. I have my brother and some of his boys on their way to meet me so we can figure out what's what. But, how do I get some hardhead niggas straight out of Brooklyn into a fancy ass casino like that?"

That was a mystery to Jordyn as well. She didn't know what type of man Bossy was, or how many people he had working with him. She knew to some extent that Bossy was very arrogant, but that was about it.

She knew a lot about arrogance, however. Thanks to Polo. If Bossy wanted Mega to work for him in order to restore his own business, there was no way he would kill him right away. Not in front of a bunch of people anyway. He was also gay, and a lot of gay men loved to keep things cute and classy. So, unless Bossy had an inside man with the Philadelphia PD, Jordyn knew Mega would be kept alive as long as he stayed inside the building.

"You said they're meeting at the grand, right?" Jordyn asked, remembering her mom's friend Jen worked there.

"Yeah. The one where all the dealers go to do business."

"I know someone who works there. It won't be hard to get your brother and his friends inside without raising any eyebrows as long as they're dressed up."

Talking to Jordyn got Mila's wheels spinning. Before speaking to her, she had no idea how they were going to get inside without a motherfucker calling the law on them. Dressing them up so that they'd be less suspicious hadn't even popped into her mind. She was glad she called Jordyn afterall.

"Thanks girl. I'll call you back in a few. Make sure you talk to your friend and let her know we'll be coming and let me know where she wants us to meet her."

"Okay. I got you. Be careful."

After hanging up with Jordyn, Mila called her brother back to ask how many men were coming with him. She also needed their pants, jacket, and shoe sizes. They had about Four hours until midnight and Rudy was already halfway there. Her plans were to rush over to a boutique and pick up some suits and loafers. Once Rudy and his crew got there they would all dress up, head over to the casino and stand guard, in case some shit popped off.

Rudy and his guys met Mila at her hotel around ten. Most of the guys she knew from the block and some of them she didn't. There were ten of them, Rudy included. She took them up to her suite, got them dressed and gave them the rundown of how her plan should go. She didn't want to draw too much attention, and didn't want Mega to know they were there, unless something went down.

"Alright y'all, no fuck ups. No drama. No bullshit." She lectured, as she went down the line of niggas and handed each of them $3,000. "We're only here as back up in case something happens. We don't need the police being called. So hit the bar, order a drink, talk to some bitches and just chill. The meeting will be taking place at the very back of the lounge, so no one needs to go back there unless need be. I'll keep my eyes on Mega and let Rudy know if I need y'all to move. My girl got one of her people to let us in through the back, so when we get there that's where y'all need to park. Don't go to the front, go straight to the back. And stay spread out."

"We got you, sis. Mega's my boy. We gon make sure he comes out this shit on top."

Although she lectured to the guys not to make any sudden moves, she was betting on shit to hit the fan. Her role in everything was to sneak up on Bossy while the men had it out with each other and put a hot one in him. He would never know what hit him. She was slick like that. No one would ever think to watch out for a beautiful bitch playing blackjack in the casino.

When they got to the Grand, Jordyn had her people already out back waiting to let them inside. Mila slid Jen Five grand for her troubles, and she and her boys walked into the casino like a madam and her freshly dressed do-boys.

Rudy had his boys spread out, two at each corner of the casino. While Mila and Rudy took seats at a blackjack table that gave them a clear visual of Bossy's section. She didn't see Mega yet, but it was still early so she relaxed and played it cool until she saw him arrive. He wouldn't be able to see her from the back of the casino, but she'd be able to see him and everything that went on.

"Ay," Rudy said, noticing her breathing a little heavy. "Relax. We got this shit. You already know I'm a crazy motherfucker so if anything pops off, I'ma light this bitch up."

"I already know." She said, giving him dap.

"Now what if nothing pops off though? How you gon get to Ru Paul back there?"

She hadn't thought about that. If Bossy did end up letting Mega walk out of the casino without accepting his offer, that didn't mean he wouldn't come after him when they got back home. All she knew was that Mega wanted Bossy dead. He hadn't told her anything other than that.

"I don't know. I guess we gotta wait and see what Mega gon do. If I see him looking stressed or something I'll go over there. I don't know what kind of deals he got in mind to make with him, so I don't wanna make a move and fuck nothing up. You know?"

"Yeah, I feel you. Well, whatever y'all got going on, me and my niggas with it. Maybe now he can see that I'm a true rider and put me on."

Mila knew that was out of the question. Mega didn't have a problem with Rudy, he actually liked him. It was just his hot headed ways that made Mega steer clear of him when it came down to business.

Chapter Twenty-Eight

Mega walked into the casino at 12:05 looking like he owned the entire block. He was dressed down in an all red suit with a white undershirt and tie to match. His shoes were shiny and crisp and his hair was slicked down like he had just gotten up from his barbers chair. He looked so good it took Mila's breath away. If it weren't for the circumstances she would've gotten up to meet him at the bar and asked if she could buy him a drink.

"There goes your boy."

"I see him." She replied, fanning herself a little.

"That nigga be fresh to death." Rudy laughed. "He look like a real boss."

"He is. That's why he wouldn't put you on. You gotta slow down, Rudy." She said, giving her little brother some cold truth. "The type of business that Mega runs is some shit you'd see in the movies. Casino. The Godfather. Bumpy Johnson. That type of shit. He can't have some hardknock, no offense, running around on his dime and his name that ends up getting his whole shit shut down. Now, I can put in a good word for you, but only if you promise me you'll get your shit together. I don't wanna see you dead or in jail behind no petty ass hustling."

"That's real, sis. And look, I been wanting more out of this street shit ever since I got off the island. All those years I sat down and wrote about how I wanted to be something. More than what I am now. I just don't have nobody to take the time out to teach me shit. So," he shrugged. "I gotta get it how I live."

His transparency made her a little sad. She knew how much of a good dude Rudy was. He never meant any harm, he just didn't know any better. She had the patience to work with that. Mega didn't. And that was just the way it was.

"I'll talk to him." She patted her brother's shoulder. "For now, let's keep our eyes open. Looks like shit's about to get real."

Mega took a seat at Bossy's table without an invitation. The crowd of men Bossy had around him all had their hands ready to go for their guns, but Mega paid neither of them any mind. He unbuttoned his jacket and crossed his legs to show his comfort in the grand scheme of things. So, if Bossy expected him to be afraid of him he had another thing coming.

"Good night to you too, Mr. Navarro." Bossy smiled and sipped from the straw in his drink.

"I don't have all night so we need to come to some type of agreement quick, fast, and in a hurry."

"Well." Bossy squealed and crossed his legs. "I love a man who can take charge. A man that knows what he wants and what he won't tolerate."

Bossy was on Mega's last nerve and he'd only been at the table for two minutes. If there weren't so many people around them he would've walked right up to the table and shot him dead. Even if that meant the police would've been looking for him. He was sick of his shit and it showed.

"What is it that you want, Bossy? I'm not working for you. I've said it a million times and quite frankly, I'm getting tired of saying it. I mean, ain't that what you gays fought for? The right to say no. The right for a motherfucker to stand up for themselves? That shit seems like a real joke right about now."

"I just don't understand why you don't want to do business with me. Am I really that hard to get along with? I think I'm a pretty fair guy. No?"

"Yeah, you are very hard to get along with. I don't need to do business with anyone other than my choosing. I built my empire alone and that's the way I plan to keep it."

Bossy immediately took offense to Mega's attitude. No one had ever spoken to him the way Mega had. He respected Mega's stance on things, he just didn't want to accept a hard no.

"I'll tell you what, Mr. Navarro." He said, tossing his napkin down onto the table. "If you do business with me for two months, I'll make it worth your while."

"Worth my while?" Mega scoffed, cutting him off. "You seem to be highly mistaken. I don't need anything from you, or anyone else in this game. You're the one who needs something from me. Worth my while would be you keeping my name off the streets and getting yourself out of whatever hole you got yourself into. My decision remains. So moving forward, how can we settle this like men?"

The feathers Mega ruffled were showing more than Bossy expected them to. He thought he would be able to threaten his opponent into accepting his offer and that would be that. He wasn't expecting Mega to go down kicking and screaming.

"A firm man I see."

"Firm in need." Mega said, uncrossing his legs to give Bossy a peek at his brass balls. "You can kill me right now, in front of all these people, but I guarantee you won't walk out of this building alive. And if you come after my family, that'd be an even bigger mistake than you've already made."

The only backup Mega had with him was Big Shaun outside with a sniper rifle. He was prepared to die that night, as long as Bossy went out with him.

"Hm." Bossy laughed a little. "You're really turning me down? Such a bold move."

Mila inched her way closer towards the lounge once she saw the conversation getting rowdy. She got close enough to be able to feel the tension and knew that she had to make a move sooner rather than later. If she waited too long to intervene, there was no question in her mind that Mega wouldn't have walked away from that table with his life.

"Sorry to interrupt." She stepped to the red velvet ropes that blocked off Bossy's section.

When Mega heard her voice his heart dropped. Mila was supposed to be on a plane back to Miami and there she was, in the casino dressed like a certified gangster's wife.

"Well!" Bossy stood up as soon as Mega did. "Who is this gorgeous ensemble joining us for a chat? Gentleman," he clapped. "Let her in. Please."

Mega looked at her like she was in big trouble. And she looked right back at him like he was too.

"What the fuck are you doing here?" he asked through clenched teeth.

"I wanted to play the slots." She smiled and took a seat at the table with them.

His heart raced in his chest. Not only did he have to get himself out of the casino alive, but Mila too. He was pissed at her for disobeying his orders, yet he understood why she did it. He had no idea what her plan was, he just hoped it was a good one.

"How are you this evening?" Bossy smiled like he had hit the jackpot.

"I'm great. Just wondering what was taking my man so long to get back to our game. Is something wrong?"

She spoke like a true Queen. Like a woman who knew her position and had been playing it for a long time. Rudy was off to the side waiting for her to give the signal, and his boys weren't too far behind ready to heat up their guns. Mila went to the table with two options in mind. Either Bossy let them walk away without an issue, or her brother was going to light his ass up like the fourth of July.

"We were just discussing some business ideas. Maybe you can be a voice of reason for him." Bossy sassed. "He seems to be under the impression that I'm asking him to accept my offer, when in fact, it is not a question. But more so a command."

Mila looked at Mega like she wanted to ask what the fuck had Bossy been smoking. And he shared the same look.

"You see, I know who you are, Ms. Mila. You took a lot of money from me and I haven't forgotten that."

"I have the money, we can settle things like adults. I'm aware that you've been offered triple what you're owed. Why not take it? Things don't have to get out of hand here."

"Out of hand?" Bossy laughed. "It seems that you two are the ones out of hand. I mean, look around you. Do you really think you can walk away from this table like nothing?"

Mila took a look at all the men he had surrounding them. There was a little fear in her heart, but when Mega touched her hand all the fear was lost. She knew her man, and her brother, would come through for her every time. So, she stood her ground. Bossy could either back off, or she would let her dogs off of their leashes. It was his call.

"Do you really think we would come here alone?" she chuckled. "You see, just like you, we have many men. The game is a game to be played. You know that." She leaned back in her chair and crossed her legs.

Mega looked around the casino to see if he could spot anyone Mila might have brought along for the ride and as soon as he laid eyes on Rudy, he already knew what time it was.

"You a cold bitch." He laughed up under his breath.

"I learned from you." She slyly replied.

Bossy grew nervous when he realized that they had people in tow as well. That was the thing about being lowkey, a motherfucker never really knew what kind of ammo you had on you. That was where Bossy always went wrong. He was so loud with his moves and the people he had guarding him, anyone could get next to him. Mega kept his shit quiet and under wraps. No one ever knew who he had riding for him, and that was the best way to play the game.

"I'm not leaving this casino without a resolution." Bossy said, calling their bluff.

Mila looked at Mega and smiled. As soon as she did, he already knew what she meant. Rudy was about to come through guns blazing and they had a cool five seconds to get the fuck out of his way.

Rudy was already rounding the front of the bar when she smiled at Mega, and once she dropped her purse on the floor he knew that meant for him and his boys to come from their corners and start shooting.

"Get down!" She shouted, when she saw Rudy come from under his jacket with his gun.

Mega wasted no time tipping both of their chairs over and crawling underneath the table. Rudy was in heaven while he let shots ring into their section. Bossy and his men didn't know what hit them. His right hand dove on top of him to shield him with his body, while everyone else went for their guns as quickly as they could.

Drinks were flying, people were screaming and running towards the exit, glass was shattering. There were so many bullets flying, Mega had no choice but to forget about Bossy and get Mila out of there as fast as he could. He wanted to risk it all and go after Bossy, but he didn't have a weapon on him, and he didn't want Mila getting hurt. One of them had to make it home to their child.

"Let's go!" He shouted over the hail of gunfire. "We gotta move! Now!"

Big Shaun was outside with his beam pointed, waiting to get a good shot at Bossy, but there was too much debris in the air for him to get a clear view. So, he started his truck and kept his eyes on the door so he could clear the scene as soon as Mega made it outside.

"Oh shit!" Mila screamed, as they rushed towards the exit with one of Bossy's men firing at them.

They had a good run right up until they made it to the metal detectors at the entrance. Bossy's man was such a good shot, he caught Mega in the shoulder, just missing Mila's head, as he pushed her through the door.

"Go! Go! Get in the car!"

Big Shaun saw Mega on the ground at the entrance and sprung right into action. He was about to run in and pull Mega out of the building, but Mega told him to grab Mila and get her to safety instead.

"Take her! Get her out of here!"

"No!" Mila kicked and screamed when Big Shaun scooped her up. "Put me down! I'm not leaving him!"

Her fight was no match for him. Big Shuan tossed her into the backseat and quickly sped off into the night.

Chapter Twenty-Nine

Mila screamed, cursed, and cried the entire time Big Shaun drove. She tried kicking out the windows and opening the doors, but none of her attempts prevailed. His truck was armored for war and he had the child locks in place so she couldn't get out. He drove until he made it thirty minutes out of the city and they both sat in silence while they waited for Mega to call.

Mila cried so hard she fell asleep in the backseat. Nearly two hours had passed and Big Shuan started to feel like Mega would never call. He started to grow nervous, the first time in years for the big man. There weren't many things that scared him, but being in the world without his best friend was at the top of the list.

When his phone finally rang, Mila immediately jumped from her slumber. Her body was so weak from fear and crying, she could barely pull herself up from the seat.

"Is it him?" She frantically asked.

"You scared me, nigga." Big Shaun let out a sigh of relief. "Where you at?"

"I'm at the hotel. Come through."

"Mega!?" She snatched the phone from Big Shaun's hand. "Are you okay!?"

"Yeah, Mila. I'm alright. You one crazy motherfucker, you know that? Thanks for having my back though."

"All the time."

She handed the big man his phone back and let herself fall back onto the seat. A smile crossed her face thinking about the shit they pulled off and although she was scared to death, she was proud of the way they handled things. They were a team. Always had been, and always would be.

As soon as they got to the hotel, Mila pressured Big Shaun to hurry up and let her out. She was mad at him for throwing her around the way he did, but she'd get over it. He was someone she'd known for a long time and she knew he never meant to hurt anybody. Unless he had to.

"I should kick your ass, you know that right?" she scolded him once he finally let her out of the car.

"I know." He laughed. "I was just doing my job."

"Mhm."

She marched up the walkway to the lobby and quickly made her way into the elevator, leaving Big Shaun to wait for it to go back down. He knew she was pissed at him, but he found it funny. He knew she would look back at things once it was all over and thank him for the way he moved. If it weren't for him, her ass would've probably been dead.

"Oh my god!" She rushed into the room when Mega opened the door and she saw blood all over his suit. "I thought you said you were okay! Where are you hit?"

"My shoulder. I think."

"You think?" she quickly started to remove his jacket as he winced in pain. "What you mean you think? Hurry up and take this off so I can see."

Big Shaun entered the room just as she was removing Mega's shirt and felt his heart skip a beat.

"You didn't say you were hit." The big man quickly locked the door and rushed to grab towels to put pressure on his friend's wounds.

"Where did it go in at? There's so much blood I can't tell."

Mila felt herself starting to panic. The sight of all the blood, on top of the tears flooding her eyes, clouded her vision so much she couldn't see.

"I felt it with my back turned." Mega said, trying his best to fight the pain of what felt like a bullet sitting inside his shoulder blade.

"No, I can't see anything." Mila said, wiping her eyes. "We need to get you to a hospital so they can find it."

Mega was strongly against going to the hospital. Mila had medical history under her belt, so he trusted her to find it. He didn't feel like the bullet went too deep, it was just small and there was so much blood it was hard to find.

Big Shaun came over with a bottle of vodka he found in the kitchen of the suite and without warning, poured it all over Mega's shoulder to clear out the blood so Mila could see. Mega groaned in pain as he held a towel over his mouth to muffle his screams.

"I see it!" She called out. "I need something to dig it out before the tissue starts to swell around it."

Big Shaun hurried and ran to the bathroom in search of a first aid kit. He remembered renting out a suite once and there being one under the kitchen sink. He checked there afterwards and there it was.

"Tweezers?"

Mila was skeptical, but with no other choice she had to put them to use.

"This is gonna have to do. It's gonna hurt, so keep that towel over your face and try to hold as still as possible."

Before she started digging into his skin, Mega poured what was left of the vodka down his throat and braced himself for what he knew he had to endure. The pain was something he'd never experienced. Every time she maneuvered the tweezers to get a better grip on the bullet, he felt like he was being shot all over again. It took her about five adjustments before she finally got a good grip and once she did, she gave a warning that she was about to pull it out.

"I think I'm gonna throw up." Big Shaun said, gagging on his own saliva. "Fuck."

"Big ass baby." She said, as she yanked the bullet from Mega's shoulder. "I'm gonna have to pack this, unless you have some needle and thread lying around somewhere."

"I'll go get some." Big Shaun quickly volunteered. "I gotta get the fuck out of here for a minute and get some fresh air."

"Get some more liquor while you at it." Mega laughed. "This shit got me blowed."

Mila packed his hole with gauze until Big Shaun made it back with the supplies she needed to stitch up Mega's shoulder. Her adrenaline was still pumping from seeing all the blood, but she was proud of herself for being able to stay calm enough to do what needed to be done. And Mega was thankful.

"You showed your ass tonight." He said, while she taped up his wound. "I appreciate that, even though you never do shit I ask you to do."

"And this is why. If I wasn't there your ass would've ended up in some shit you didn't wanna be in."

"True." He nodded. "Rudy and his boys make it back to Brooklyn?"

"I don't know. My phone died at the casino. I bet they did though. My brother ain't nothing to be fucked with."

"Hell yeah. I owe that boy my life."

"He just really wanna be down." She sighed, getting up to clean herself up. "I told him I'd talk to you about it, but he has to change the way he moves first."

Mega sat in silence, admiring Mila from across the room. He was impressed. The way she came through for him that night made him see her in a different light. She really proved herself to him and he was more than grateful to her. However, as far as their intimate relationship, he didn't know where they stood.

"You wanna smoke?" he asked, getting up to meet her in the kitchen.

"Hell yeah. My nerves are bad fucking with you."

"I got some fire ass weed from the southside. This shit smoking."

He lit the blunt, took a few puffs and handed it off to her. If there was anybody Mega loved to smoke with, it was Mila. Whenever they got high together there were nothing but laughs and good conversations. Good food too, when she was in the mood to cook.

He missed his smoking partner. He missed laughing with her. Hanging out and kicking back. When he thought about it, Mila was really one of his best friends. Someone he could confide in. someone who always had his back. They both made a lot of mistakes during their relationship, but one thing was for certain, they never turned their backs on each other. Ever.

"Why you looking at me like that?" she nearly blushed.

"I don't know." He smiled and lowered his head. "Just thinking bout how goofy we used to be whenever we smoked."

"Nah," she laughed. "How goofy you would be. You have no sense at all when you high."

"Good vibes, man. Good vibes."

Mila felt like their vibes were always good. Even if they were mad at each other. There was something in the air between them, other than smoke, that night. And she couldn't resist. Before he could say another word about their good times, she walked right up to him and kissed him.

Her kiss was so full of passion he couldn't pull away. Instead, he picked her up, wrapped her legs around his waist and kissed her back. Before he knew it they were down on the couch doing all the freaky things they used to do. In the back of his mind he kept telling himself to stop, but he was too far gone. The liquor. The weed. Both of their adrenalines. The only thing Mega was conscious enough to remember to do was pull out, before he got her pregnant again.

"We shouldn't have done that." She said, feeling a little guilty.

"I know." He replied, resting his head on her chest. "Fuck."

When he heard his phone start to ring he already knew who it was. He was ashamed to answer it at first, but knew he had to. If not, Jordyn would only keep calling until she knew that he was okay.

"Answer it." Mila said, nudging him off of her. "She needs to know that you're okay. I'm gonna go to my room and shower."

"Alright. Be up by 7. Our flight leaves in a few hours."

"Yeah."

Mila was hurt. Most of all, she was mad at herself for being so caught up in the moment. She felt bad for having sex with Mega knowing that he had Jordyn waiting for them back home. That wasn't the type of woman she wanted to be anymore. Especially not to Jordyn. She deserved so much more than that.

When she got to her room all she could do was cry. And after a while of thinking about the situation between her and Mega, she felt the need to get it off her chest. She wanted to come clean to Jordyn, woman to woman, that way he couldn't put all the blame on her. But, decided it wasn't her place. That was something Mega owed her.

Chapter Thirty

Aside from her morning sickness, Jordyn had a funny feeling in her gut. She'd tossed and turned all night and couldn't focus on anything other than Mega. She couldn't help but feel like there was something he wasn't telling her. Nonetheless, she was excited to finally have him home and have everything put behind them.

When she saw him and Mila walking down the gate she wanted to puke again. They looked like they'd had a long night. Like something other than taking care of Bossy was eating away at their conscience. If there was any look Jordyn knew all too well, it was the look of guilt. And both of them looked guilty as hell.

"Morning." Mega approached her and kissed her head.

"Hey." She replied, unsure of how to feel.

He reached for MJ, who was still asleep on Jordyn's shoulder, and hugged her tight. Mila stood in front of them rubbing MJ's back and kissing her tiny arms and hands, while Jordyn stood off to the side feeling like an outcast. She wanted to walk off, but didn't want the ride home to be awkward, so she just stood there. Waiting for their little family reunion to be over with.

"Let's get out of here." Mila said, noticing Jordyn's awkwardness.

When Mega realized why she said that he quickly moved his feet and headed for the exit. Mila let him walk ahead of her and asked Jordyn to stay behind so they could talk. She wanted to thank her again for taking care of her daughter, and also see if she'd be able to pick up on her mood.

"You okay?" she asked, rubbing Jordyn's shoulder. "You look tired."

"I couldn't sleep for shit last night and woke up this morning feeling sick."

Mila knew the feeling. She woke up feeling sick every morning while she was pregnant with MJ. She also knew the look Jordyn had on her face. There was something different in her eyes that morning. Something more mature. Mila couldn't tell whether it was because of what happened at the casino that night, or if she was pregnant.

"Morning sickness huh?" Mila asked, in a motherly way. "Is that all it is?"

Jordyn tried hard to hide her smile. She felt like Mila already knew where her morning sickness was stemming from, and she was acting pretty cool about it. For some reason, that made her feel better than she did when she got up that morning.

"Don't say anything to Mega yet. Please." Jordyn blushed. "I wanna tell him once we're all settled down and shit."

"I won't." Mila smiled and put her arm around Jordyn. "Now let's get out of here. I'm tired as hell and wanna spend some time with my baby."

Mega and MJ were already in the car ready to go when they finally made it outside. His face was flushed with nervousness when Jordyn looked at him. He'd barely even looked at her one time since they got there. She tried to put it off on him being injured, but her logic told her otherwise.

She pulled up to drop Mila off before they went home. Mega got out to help her with MJ and her bags, and Jordyn waited in the car. She was so anxious about whatever it was she felt in her gut, she had to call Kaylani.

"Hey, baby girl." Kaylani answered on the first ring.

"Girl." Jordyn said, sounding like she wanted to cry.

"Oh Lord, I know that tone. What happened?"

Before she could even get her words out, the tears started to pour. Jordyn cried so hard, Kaylani was ready to pull up wherever she was and get some straightening.

"What is it, Jordyn? What's wrong?"

"I don't know." She cried. "I'm just so emotional. I feel like Mega did something and isn't telling me about it."

"Something like what?"

Kaylani was ready to snap. After everything Jordyn had done for him. Putting her life on the line. Doing shit she wouldn't normally do. Getting involved with criminal activity. Taking care of his kid. Her leg started to shake while she waited for Jordyn to say whatever it was she had to say.

"We're at Mila's house now, dropping her and the baby off. I just picked them up from the airport. I know he fucked her last night. I know he did. I couldn't sleep. Tossed and turned all night. And today he can't even look me in my face."

Kaylani let out a long sigh. Although she tried her hardest to give Jordyn good advice and give Mega a chance, she knew it was only a matter of time before she came crying to her about him and Mila.

"And on top of that, I found out that I'm pregnant."

The phone grew silent. Kaylani was completely speechless. As many times as they had talked about waiting until marriage before they ever had kids, she couldn't believe what Jordyn had told her. She was pissed.

"You're pregnant?"

"I already know what you're gonna say." Jordyn rolled her eyes. "I didn't plan on any of this happening. I guess I was just so caught up in the moment I neglected to be careful."

"Jordyn." Kaylani sighed. "Are you serious right now? And then you find out this nigga still sleeping with his baby mama? Come on. You know better than this. You were on and off with Polo's ass for years and never got pregnant by him."

"I know." She started to cry again. "That's what makes me so mad at myself. Here I am being a good ass bitch. A down ass bitch. Doing shit that I would never do and he does me like this? I can't. Why me? What's wrong with me?"

"Aww." Kaylani felt her heart breaking. "There's nothing wrong with you. You're perfect. Niggas just can't keep their dicks in their pants. Come to my house. We'll figure this shit out."

"I love you. Meet me at his house. I have to get my shit."

Mega saw her hanging up the phone and wiping her eyes on his way back to the car. When he got inside she tried to put the car in reverse and act like nothing was wrong, but he stopped her.

"You know, don't you?" he asked, feeling ashamed of himself.

"I do. I saw it on your face the moment you stepped off the plane."

Mega was mad at himself. When he saw the tears streaming down her face he hated himself even more. His heart broke in the passenger seat of that car and he was scared he would lose Jordyn forever.

"I'm sorry. I didn't mean for it to happen. I won't sit here and make any excuses for myself. I just hope that you can forgive me."

Jordyn's heart was hurting, and as fucked up as Mega was for doing what he did, she still yearned for him. She still wanted to love him. He made no excuses for himself, but in her mind she had every excuse in the world for him. What pissed her off even more than what Mega had done, was the fact that Mila had smiled in her face, knowing what they'd done the whole time.

"I'm having Kaylani pick me up when we get back. I need time to clear my mind and make some sense of this."

"What?" Mega frowned. "Why you gotta go over there?"

"Mega, you cheated on me. What the fuck? Not only that, but I'm pregnant. Here I am doing all this shit for you. Taking care of your kid. Helping this bitch come up with a plan to get you out of trouble. And I'm pregnant. Not even thinking about myself and you could still do me like that?" She snapped. "That's fucked up. As much as I love you, I'm fully prepared to take care of my baby on my own, because one thing I'm not going to do is have my child around bullshit."

He didn't know what to say after finding out she was pregnant. Honestly, that was all he heard her say. She was ranting and raving behind the wheel and all he'd heard her say was that she was pregnant. It was a terrible time, but Mega was happy. After his night with Mila he realized that Jordyn was the one he really wanted to be with. He was in love with her. And the fact that she was pregnant with his baby made him fall even harder.

Made in the USA
Columbia, SC
13 October 2023

24419428R00163